GOBLIN SLAYER

©Noboru Kannatuki

"Goblin Slayer."

"None to speak of."

"Welcome back!
    Are you all right?
        No major injuries?"

DWARF SHAMAN

"Before they're polished, jewels and precious metals all look like rocks. No dwarf would judge a thing by its appearance alone."

HIGH ELF ARCHER

"Ignorance is bliss, for learning is the highest joy."
—Elven proverb

LIZARD PRIEST

"A Naga..."

GOBLIN SLAYER

HE DOES NOT LET
ANYONE
ROLL THE DICE.

CHARACTER
PROFILES

©Noboru Kannatuki

PRIESTESS

"Protect, heal, save."
Three Holy Tenets of the Earth Mother

GOBLIN SLAYER

"I am to goblins what goblins are to us."

GUILD GIRL

"How can you go adventuring
without pen and paper?"

COW GIRL

The only things that matter to her
are the weather, the animals, the crops…and him.

Contents

©Noboru Kannatuki

GOBLIN SLAYER

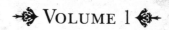

❖ VOLUME 1 ❖

KUMO KAGYU

Illustration by
NOBORU KANNATUKI

YEN
ON

NEW YORK

GOBLIN SLAYER

KUMO KAGYU

Translation by Kevin Steinbach ✣ Cover art by Noboru Kannatuki

GOBLIN SLAYER vol. 1
Copyright © 2016 Kumo Kagyu
Illustrations copyright © 2016 Noboru Kannatuki
All rights reserved.
Original Japanese edition published in 2016 by SB Creative Corp.
This English edition is published by arrangement with SB Creative Corp., Tokyo, in care of Tuttle-Mori Agency, Inc., Tokyo.

English translation © 2016 by Yen Press, LLC

Yen On
1290 Avenue of the Americas
New York, NY 10104

Visit us at yenpress.com ✣ facebook.com/yenpress ✣ twitter.com/yenpress
yenpress.tumblr.com ✣ instagram.com/yenpress

First Yen On Edition: December 2016

Yen On is an imprint of Yen Press, LLC.
The Yen On name and logo are trademarks of Yen Press, LLC.

Library of Congress Cataloging-in-Publication Data
Names: Kagyū, Kumo, author. | Kannatuki, Noboru, illustrator.
Title: Goblin slayer / Kumo Kagyu ; illustration by Noboru Kannatuki.
Other titles: Goburin sureiyā. English
Description: New York, NY : Yen On, 2016–
Identifiers: LCCN 2016033529 | ISBN 9780316501590 (v. 1 : paperback)
Subjects: LCSH: Goblins—Fiction. | GSAFD: Fantasy fiction.
Classification: LCC PL872.5.A367 G6313 2016 | DDC 895.63/6—dc23
LC record available at https://lccn.loc.gov/2016033529

ISBN: 978-0-316-50159-0 (paperback)
      978-0-316-55324-7 (ebook)

10 9 8 7 6 5 4 3 2 1

LSC-C

Printed in the United States of America

Once upon a time, in the days when the stars shone far fewer in the sky than they do now...

The gods of light and order and destiny vied with the gods of darkness and chaos and chance to see who would control the world. This struggle took place, not in battle, but with a roll of the dice.

Or rather, many, many rolls. Again and again and again they rolled the dice.

And there were victories, and there were defeats, but there was no resolution.

At long last, the gods tired of dice. Thereupon they created many creatures to be their playing pieces and a world in which to play. Humans and elves and dwarves and lizardmen, goblins and ogres and trolls and demons.

At times they adventure, sometimes gaining victory, other times suffering defeat. They find treasure, become happy, and in the end, they die.

Into this world, there appeared one particular adventurer.
He will not save the world.
He will not even change anything.
After all, he is just another pawn, such as you might find anywhere...

CHAPTER 1

THE FATE OF SOME ADVENTURERS

The brutal fight over, he ground his boot into slain goblin's cadaver.

He was stained crimson with the monster's blood, from his grimy steel helm and leather armor to the mail made of chain-linked metal rings that covered his entire body.

A small, battered shield was fastened to his left arm, and in one hand, he held a brightly burning torch.

Heel braced against the creature's corpse, he reached down with his free hand and casually withdrew his sword from its skull. It was a cheap-looking blade, its length poorly conceived, and now it was drenched in the goblin's brains.

Lying on the ground, an arrow in her shoulder, the young girl's thin frame shook with fear. Her sweet, classically lovely face framed by long hair almost a translucent gold was scrunched up into a mess of tears and sweat.

Her slim arms, her feet—her whole gorgeous body was clad in the vestments of a priestess. The sounding staff she clutched jangled, the rings hanging on it striking one another in time with the quaking of her hands.

Who was this man before her?

So strange was his appearance, the aura that cloaked him, that she imagined he might be a goblin himself—or perhaps something far worse, something she had no knowledge of yet.

"Wh-who are you…?" she asked, pushing down her terror and pain.

After a pause, the man answered, "Goblin Slayer."

A killer. Not of dragons or vampires, but the lowliest of monsters: goblins.

Normally, the name might have seemed comically simple. But to Priestess, at that moment, it was anything but funny.

§

You've heard this one before.

The day an orphan raised in the Temple turns fifteen, they become an adult and must choose their path: Will they remain in the Temple as a servant of the goddess, or will they leave and try to make their way in the greater world?

Priestess had chosen the latter, and a visit to the Adventurers Guild was how she had chosen to do it.

The Adventurers Guild—created to support those courageous questing souls—was first formed, so it was said, by a handful of people who met one another in a bar. Unlike other workers' associations, the Adventurers Guild was less a labor union than an employment agency. In the ongoing war between the monsters and "those who have language," adventurers were like mercenaries. No one would tolerate the existence of armed toughs if they were not managed carefully.

Priestess stopped in her tracks as the vast branch office that stood directly inside the town gates took her breath away. When she entered the lobby, she was taken aback to find it bustling with adventurers, even though it was still morning.

These buildings boasted large inns and taverns—usually together—as well as a business office, all in one. Really, this kind of clamor was the natural result of providing these three services in one place.

For every ordinary human in plate armor, there was an elven mage with staff and mantle. Here there was a bearded, ax-wielding dwarf; there, one of the little meadow-dwelling folk known as rheas. Priestess wound her way through the crowd, past males and females of every race and age imaginable carrying every possible type of weapon, toward Guild Girl. The line snaked on and on, full of people who had come to take on or lodge a quest or to file a report.

A spear-wielding adventurer was chatting with one covered in heavy armor.

"And? How was the manticore in the pass?"

"It wasn't much. If you want a big one, I think you'd better try the ruins or something."

"Fair enough, but you're never gonna put food on the table that way."

"Hey, I've heard there's an evil spirit making trouble up near the Capital. Whoever goes over there might be in for a nice payday, hey?"

"Maybe I could handle it, if it's just some low-level demon…"

Priestess was brought up short no less than three times listening to their casual conversation, and each time she pulled her sounding staff close to herself to steel her resolve.

"…Soon I will also…!"

She had no illusions that an adventurer's lot was an easy one. Priestess had seen firsthand the wounded return from the dungeon, coming to the Temple, begging for a healing miracle. And healing such people was precisely the creed of the Earth Mother.

How could she shrink away, then, from putting herself in danger to do as she had been taught? She was an orphan, and the Temple had saved her. And now it was her turn to repay that debt…

"Yes, what brings you here today?"

The line had steadily moved along while Priestess stood lost in thought, and now it was her turn.

Wearing a gentle expression, Guild Girl attending her was a girl, still young, but older than Priestess. Her immaculate outfit was impeccably kept, her light brown hair woven into braids. A quick glance around the hall left no doubt the guild front desk would be a demanding place to work. That the receptionist showed none of the strained demeanor all too common among professional young women was perhaps a sign of how well she knew her job.

Priestess felt a bit of her nervousness ebb. She swallowed and spoke up.

"Uh, I…I want to be an…an adventurer."

"Is that…right?" Guild Girl asked, her sweet expression momentarily slipping as she hesitated briefly, seemingly at a loss for words. Priestess felt the receptionist's eyes moving from her face down her body, and strangely embarrassed, she nodded.

The feeling faded as Guild Girl reassumed a smile and said, "I see. Can you read and write?"

"Um, yes, a little. I learned at the Temple…"

"Then fill this out, please. If there's anything you don't understand, just ask."

It was an Adventure Sheet. Gold letters paraded across the light brown vellum.

Name, sex, age, class, hair color, eye color, body type, skills, spells, miracles… Such simple information. So simple it almost didn't seem right.

"Oh," Guild Girl broke in, "you can leave the 'Abilities' and 'Adventure History' spots blank. The guild will fill those in later."

"Y-yes, ma'am." Priestess nodded, and then with a quivering hand, she picked up a pen, dipped it in an inkpot, and began writing in precise letters.

She handed the finished sheet to Guild Girl, who looked it over with a nod, then took a silver stylus and carved a series of flowing letters into a white porcelain tile. She passed the tile to Priestess, who discovered it bore the same information as her Adventure Sheet in closely spaced letters.

"This will serve as your identification. We call it your 'Status.' Although," she added teasingly, "it doesn't say anything we can't figure out by looking at you." Then she calmly told the blinking Priestess, "It will be used to corroborate your identity if anything happens to you, so try not to lose it."

If anything happens?

For a second, Priestess was caught off guard by Guild Girl's businesslike tone, but it didn't take her long to connect the dots. The only time they might need to "corroborate your identity" was when you'd been murdered so horrifically no one could tell who you were.

"Yes, ma'am," Priestess said, and she wished her voice would stop shaking. "But is it really this easy to become an adventurer…?"

"To *become* one, yes."

The other girl's expression was unreadable. Was she worried or perhaps resigned? Priestess couldn't tell.

"It's harder to move up the ranks. That's based on kills, how much good you've done, and personality tests."

"Personality tests?"

"Sometimes you get the I'm-strong-enough-to-do-it-all-by-myself types."

Then, under her breath, she added, "But there are all kinds of eccentrics out there." And when she said it, for an instant her demeanor changed. Softened into a warm, wistful smile.

Oh, Priestess thought, *I didn't realize she could smile like that.*

Guild Girl noticed Priestess watching her and hastily cleared her throat. "Quests are posted over there." She indicated a corkboard that covered almost an entire wall. "Choose ones that are appropriate to your level, of course."

Pickings were slim, since the huge crowd of adventurers had been going over the board all morning. But the Guild wouldn't have a board that size if they didn't need it.

"Personally," the receptionist said, "I'd recommend getting your feet wet by cleaning the sewers. No pun intended."

"Cleaning the sewers? I thought adventurers fought monsters…?"

"There's honor in hunting giant rats, too. And you'll be doing some real good in the world." She added under her breath, "Newcomers with a little experience could move on to goblins, I guess," and there was that wordless look again.

"Well, that's it for registration. Happy hunting!"

"Oh, th-thank you." Priestess ducked her head in gratitude and left the front desk. She hung the porcelain tablet around her neck and let out a breath she had been holding. She was a registered adventurer. It was just that simple.

But what am I supposed to do now?

Priestess carried only her staff (the symbol of her office), a bag with a change of clothes, and a few coins.

She had heard the second floor of the Guild building was aimed at low-level adventurers. Maybe she should start by reserving a room, then see what kinds of quests were available…

"Hey, wanna go adventuring with us?"

"Wuuuh?"

The unexpected invitation came from a young man with a sword at his hip and a shiny breastplate tied to his chest. Like Priestess, he had a brand-new porcelain tablet around his neck.

The tablets came in ten varieties indicating the rank of the wearer, from platinum at the top to the porcelain of newly minted adventurers at the very bottom.

"You're a priestess, right?"

"Um, yes. Yes…I am."

"Perfect! Exactly what my party needs."

Just past the young swordsman, she could now see two other girls. One wore a martial artist's uniform, her hair in a bundle and a confident look in her eye, while the other had a staff and glasses, wearing a cool gaze.

A fighter and a wizard, she guessed.

Warrior followed her glance and repeated, "My party," with a nod. "We're on an urgent quest, but I'd like at least one more person. How about you?"

"What do you mean, 'urgent'…?"

"We're gonna get rid of some goblins!"

Goblins. Goblins had been living in the caves near town since time immemorial, or so it was said. They were the weakest of the monsters, and sheer numbers were the only thing acting in their favor.

They stood about as tall as a child, with strength and wits to match. All that distinguished them from a small human was their ability to see in the dark. They did all the usual monster things—threaten people, terrorize villages, kidnap maidens.

They were weak, yes, but it was better to let sleeping goblins lie.

The villagers had ignored the goblins at first…but then things changed. First, the crops they had stored up for winter disappeared, down to the last seed. The enraged townspeople mended the fences, then set patrols outside with torches in hand.

The goblins promptly slipped past them.

They stole the sheep, along with the shepherd's daughter and some womenfolk who came out to see what all the fuss was about.

The villagers were quickly running out of options. They marshaled their meager resources and went to the Guild—the Adventurers Guild, where the adventurers gathered. Surely, posting a quest would bring someone to help.

Um, and…

Priestess stood with a finger to her lips, lost in thought as Warrior reeled off his explanation.

A good old-fashioned goblin hunt for her first adventure. Lots of people had done that. And she hadn't even needed to find the adventure—the adventure had found her. It had to be fate.

She had never imagined she could do it all herself, anyway. Soloing as a cleric was suicide. She was going to need a party eventually. She was very worried about joining up with total strangers—but someone who had extended an invitation to her wasn't quite a *total* stranger, was he? True, no boy had ever invited her to anything before, but there were two other girls there.

So it would be fine…right?

"All right, then. If you'll have me."

She replied with a firm nod, and Warrior gave a whoop.

"Really?! Awesome! Now, who's ready to go on an adventure?!"

"What, just the four of you?" Guild Girl broke in. "I'm sure if you wait a while, some other adventurers will show up…"

It didn't seem to bother Warrior that Guild Girl herself had felt the need to comment. "It's just some goblins. I'm sure four people is plenty." He turned to his companions. "Right?" He sounded so sure, a cheerful smile on his face. Then he turned back to Guild Girl. "Those captured maidens are waiting to be rescued. There's no time to lose!"

Seeing this, the young worker's face settled back into that unreadable expression while a profound and strange unease took hold deep in Priestess's heart.

§

The torch flickered dishearteningly in the putrid breeze.

The midday sun was blotted out by the darkness that filled the cave. At the opening, it was hard to see, and farther in, it was almost black.

The shadows of the jutting rough-hewn rocks danced in time with the bobbing flame, sliding along the walls like monsters in a fresco.

Three girls and one boy, covered in whatever poor pieces of armor they could find. In spotty formation, they picked their way nervously through the thick darkness. Warrior went on point, holding the torch. Their Fighter was behind him. Wizard held the rear guard. And sandwiched in between the martial artist and the magician, third in line, was the young woman in priestess's robes, clutching her sounding staff anxiously as she walked.

It was Wizard who had suggested they travel in a line. So long as there were no branching paths, they wouldn't have to worry about an attack from behind. And if the adventurers in front held fast, those behind would be safe, able to provide support from the back ranks. That was the plan, anyway.

"I-is this really a good idea? Jumping right in?" Priestess's murmur hardly sounded confident. If anything, she sounded considerably more concerned than she had before they'd entered the cave. "I mean, we don't know anything about these goblins."

"Sheesh, what a worrywart. I guess that's just what you can expect from a priestess." Warrior's voice, a bit too bold in the emptiness of the cave, echoed until it disappeared. "Even kids aren't afraid of goblins. Heck, I helped drive some out of my village once."

"Oh, stop," Fighter said. "Killing a few goblins is nothing special. You're embarrassing yourself. And," she added in a disagreeable but low voice, "you didn't even *kill* them."

"I didn't say I did," Warrior responded with a pout.

Fighter gave an annoyed but somehow affectionate sigh. "They might chop this loser into lunch meat, but I'll send 'em flying. So don't worry."

"Loser? That hurts!" The torchlight shone on Warrior's dejected face, but the next moment, he was gleefully hoisting his sword. "Hey, the four of us, we could handle a dragon if we had to!"

"My, aren't we eager?" Wizard muttered, causing Fighter to giggle. The group's echoing voices mingled in the cavern.

Priestess kept silent, as if afraid talking would attract something from the darkness.

"But I do hope to hunt a dragon someday," Wizard said. "Don't you?" Priestess's wordless smile seemed to agree with Wizard and the nodding Warrior. But the darkness hid an expression as ambiguous as Guild Girl's.

Do we really? she asked herself, but she dared not voice her doubts, even as the unease built to a storm within her.

"*The four of us could…*," he'd said, but how could he so completely trust people he'd hardly known two whole days? Priestess knew these weren't bad people, but…

"Are you sure we shouldn't have prepared a little more?" she pressed. "We don't even have any p-p…potions."

"We don't have any money, either. Or time to shop, for that matter," Warrior answered with bravado, paying no heed to the tremble in Priestess's voice. "I'm worried about those kidnapped girls… And anyway, if one of us gets hurt, you can just heal us, right?"

"It's true I have the miracles of healing and light…but…"

"Then we'll be fine!"

No one could have heard Priestess say thickly, "But I can only use them three times…"

"It's great you're so confident and all," Fighter said, "but are you sure we won't get lost?"

"It's one long tunnel. How could we possibly get lost?"

"I don't know about that. You get so carried away. I can't take my eyes off you for two seconds!"

"Look who's talking…"

Fighter and Warrior, who came from the same hometown, slipped into one of the friendly arguments they had shared since the start of the journey.

Priestess, trailing behind them, clung to her staff with both hands and repeated the name of the Earth Mother under her breath.

"Please, see us safely through this…"

She prayed so softly her words didn't even echo, only dropping into the darkness and disappearing.

Perhaps the Earth Mother heard her prayer, or perhaps Priestess had simply been exceptionally attentive as she said the words.

"Come on, hurry up. Keep up the line," Wizard chided her.

"Oh, right, sorry…"

©Noboru Kannatuki

It was Priestess who noticed it first.

She was just walking by Wizard, who had overtaken her while she was praying, when she heard it. A scuttling sound, like a rolling pebble.

Priestess gave a start.

"Again? What is it this time?" Wizard asked in annoyance as she once more overtook Priestess, who stood quivering in place.

Wizard had graduated at the top of her class from the academy in the Capital where she had learned her spells, and she was not very fond of priestesses. The skittish little girl in their party had made an abysmal first impression, and since entering the cave, Wizard's estimation of her had only gotten worse.

"J-just now, I thought I heard something c-crumbling..."

"Where? In front of us?"

"N-no, behind us..."

Oh, please.

This wasn't caution; it was cowardice. This priestess didn't have the guts to take her life in her hands the way an adventurer needed to. Warrior and Fighter kept getting farther ahead as she stood there. Caught up in their banter, the two of them never looked back.

An ever more distant light behind them and only deepening darkness before, Wizard heaved a sigh.

"Look. We've been going straight as an arrow since we entered this cave, right? What could possibly be behi—" And then her cool, exasperated tone—

"Goblins!!"

—became a scream.

It wasn't crumbling Priestess had heard, but digging.

Hideous creatures jumped out of a tunnel and flocked toward Wizard, who had the misfortune of being last in line.

Every hand held a crude weapon, every face a repulsive look. These were the child-sized cave dwellers.

Goblins.

"G-g-gggg..."

Suddenly unable to find her voice, Wizard raised the garnet-tipped staff she had received at graduation.

It was a miracle her twisted tongue was able to form the words of the spell.

"*Sagitta...inflammarae...radius!*" Arrow of flame, emerge!

As she pulled each piece of the spell from where it had been carved deep into her memory, the words began welling up—words with the power to mold reality itself.

A glowing, arrow-shaped Firebolt flew from the fist-sized garnet on her staff and struck a goblin in the face. There was a stomach-turning sizzle and the stench of searing flesh.

That's one down!

The victory brought a rush of exhilaration that left an incongruous smile on her face. It filled Wizard with the confidence that what worked once would work again.

"*Sagitta...inflammarae...radi*aaaghhh!!"

But there were many goblins and only four party members. Before she could finish the spell, one of the little foes grabbed her arm. She didn't even have time to respond before the goblin slammed her to the coarse stone floor.

"Argh! Uh—!"

Her glasses were thrown from her face and shattered on the ground, leaving her vision blurry. A goblin quickly plucked her staff from her hand.

"H-hey! Give that back! That's not for the likes of y-you!"

A magical conduit such as a staff or a ring was a spell caster's lifeline, but more than that, it was her pride.

As if in answer to Wizard's half-mad shout, the goblin held the staff in front of her eyes and broke it with a *crack*.

Wizard's face twisted in rage, her mask of detachment gone.

"Why, you—!"

She writhed on the ground, struggling against her captor with her weak arms, her ample chest bouncing. It was not a wise choice. The irritated goblin took his dagger and drove it hard into her stomach.

"Hrrrghh?!" She gave an agonized cry as the blade pierced her innards.

Of course, Wizard's companions were not idle, not even Priestess.

"H-hey, all of you! Get away from her! Stop—!" She waved her staff about with her delicate arms, trying to chase the goblins away.

There are those clerics who are skilled in the martial arts. Some, having adventured for a long time, might even boast a good deal of physical strength.

Priestess was not one of them.

The way she was frantically swinging her staff, she wouldn't have hit anything, anyway.

Each time her sounding staff struck a wall or the ground, it made a rattling noise. And for better or for worse, the goblins took a step back.

Perhaps they took her for a warrior priestess, or maybe they were just afraid she might hit one of them through sheer luck.

Whatever the reason, Priestess took advantage of the momentary opening to pull Wizard away from them.

"Be strong!" Priestess shouted, almost shaking Wizard. "Hang on—!"

But there was no answer. Priestess's hand came away soaked with blood.

The rusty blade was still buried in Wizard's abdomen, the cruel tear revealing her ravaged entrails.

Priestess felt her throat close at the awful sight, her breath coming in a strained squeak.

"Ah...Agh..."

But Wizard was alive. Twitching and convulsing, but alive.

There was still time. There had to be. Priestess bit hard on her lip.

Clasping her staff close to her chest, Priestess placed her hand on Wizard's spilling viscera as if to push them back into place and recited the words of the miracle.

"O Earth Mother, abounding in mercy, lay your revered hand upon this child..."

Magic spells can affect the rational workings of the world, but Minor Heal is genuine divine intervention.

As the prayer took hold, Priestess's palm began glowing with a soft light that floated over to Wizard. As the light began to bubble away, Wizard's ruined stomach gradually stitched itself back together.

Of course, the goblins were not the kind to stand by and just let this happen.

"Damn you! You filthy goblins! How dare you do this to everyone!!"

Warrior had finally noticed what was going on behind him and came flying through to cover his companions, cutting off their would-be attackers.

He had thrown away the torch and now gripped his sword firmly in both hands. He gave a thrust, piercing a goblin's throat.

"GUIA?!"

"Who's next?"

He wrenched the sword from his first victim, catching a second as he turned. He sliced the goblin clean from shoulder to hip.

Through a geyser of goblin blood, Warrior gave a great shout, drunk with bloodlust.

"Well, what's wrong?! Come and get me!"

Warrior was the second son of a farmer, and since his youth, he had dreamed of becoming a knight. How one might go about becoming a knight, he did not know, but he was certain strength was a prerequisite. The knights in the bedtime stories he'd heard were always vanquishing monsters, thwarting evil, and saving the world. Here in this cave—striking down these goblins, saving helpless maidens, and protecting his friends—he saw himself a knight at last.

The thought brought a smile to his face.

Power coursed through his hands, his blood pounded in his ears, everything narrowed until he could see only the enemy before him.

"Wait! You can't handle them alone!"

He was not yet a real knight.

Even as Fighter's voice reached him, Warrior found one of the goblins' worn swords buried in his thigh.

"Ngah! Why, you—!"

It was the goblin he had cut across the chest. Warrior's blood-dulled blade had not been enough to make a killing blow.

Thrown out of his fighting posture, Warrior dealt a second blow to the goblin, and this time it died without so much as a gurgle.

But a moment later, another monster was leaping up behind him…

"Take *this*!" He made to counter with his sword, but it struck the cave wall with a blunt thud.

It was the last move he would ever make.

The torch he had dropped on the ground sputtered and died, and in the darkness that pressed in suddenly around him, he was amazed how loudly his scream echoed.

With no pedigree and no money, Warrior had been unable to afford a shield or helm; he had only his thin chest plate to protect him. He had no way to save himself from the goblins' vicious blows.

"No…it can't be!"

Fighter had failed to reach the enemy in time. As she watched the young man she thought of so fondly die, she went pale and stood stock-still.

It was all she could do to form her two trembling hands into fists and take a fighting stance.

"You two, run."

"B-but…!" Priestess protested weakly, but she knew it was useless. Despite the ministrations of Minor Heal, Wizard in her arms was barely responsive, her breath coming in short, shallow gasps.

The horde of goblins was creeping closer, fixed on its remaining prey. They were still cautious of Fighter, but they would be upon her before long.

Priestess looked at Wizard and Fighter, and then she stared in horror at the goblins still abusing the body of the fallen Warrior.

Seeing that her companions still hadn't moved, Fighter gave a click of her tongue. Then she let out a loud, clear yell, charging into the crowd of monsters.

"Hi-yaaaaah!"

Her fists and feet were limber and quick. Her own father had trained her before he died, and now she showed the very essence of his art.

She would not die here. Her father's art could not lose to such pitiful foes.

So long as I live, I will never forgive them for killing that boy!

Heart and mind bore out her training as she drove her fist into a goblin's solar plexus.

She pushed her enemy to the side as he fell vomiting to the floor, then caught him with a single knifehand strike to the neck as she spun.

Critical hit.

The immense blow to the neck left the goblin's head leaning at an impossible angle as it collapsed.

At the same moment, she stepped into the space left by his body and used the momentum to throw an arcing kick into the air in front of her. Her tightly controlled roundhouse caught two more goblins, killing them before they hit the ground—

"Wha—?!"

But a third goblin easily caught her leg and trapped her ankle.

Fighter's face paled as he began to squeeze.

Goblins were supposed to be the size of children…weren't they?

"HUURRRRGH!"

The creature, whose rancid breath washed over her as it strained itself, was giant.

She was not a small girl, and even she had to raise her head to look this enemy in the eye. The pain in her foot grew worse and worse until it wrenched a cry from her lips.

"Ahh…a-arrrrgh…let…me…go-aaah!!"

Fighter's leg still in his grip, the goblin casually rammed her up against the wall. There was a distant, dry sound of something cracking.

Fighter passed out without so much as a whimper, so she was unaware as the goblin whipped her around and slammed her against the opposite wall.

"Hrr, guhhh…?!"

She came to with a sound that was barely human, her vomit tinged with blood as she was thrown to the ground. Then the rest of the horde fell on her.

"Agh! Urrgh! Ya…yaaah! Ugh!"

The goblins beat Fighter with their clubs, deaf to her cries, until her clothes ripped and fell away with the relentless flailing.

The goblins showed as much mercy to the invading adventurers as the party had intended to show to them.

Racked by her horrific ordeal, Fighter gave a high, piercing scream, but within it, Priestess was sure she could make out words.

"Run! Hurry!"

"I—I'm sorry…!"

Closing her ears to the echoes in the cavern of the goblins violating her companion, Priestess hefted Wizard and began a stumbling retreat.

Run. Run. Run. Trip, then catch yourself, and run even harder.

Through the dark she went, slipping on every stone but never stopping.

"I'm sorry…! I'm…sorry! Please fo…forgive me…!" The words fell out of her in ragged gasps.

There was no light anymore. She knew they were being chased deeper and deeper into the cave, but what could she do?

"Ahh...ah..."

The footsteps of the goblins, drawing nearer with every echo, were what terrified her most.

Stopping now would be foolish, and she couldn't head back the way she came. Even if she could, she wouldn't have seen anything for the gloom.

Now she understood the Guild receptionist's ambiguous expression.

Yes, goblins were weak. Their party of eager adventurers—their Warrior, their Wizard, their Fighter—had known that. Goblins were about as large and smart and strong as a human child. Just as they'd heard.

But what happened when children took up weapons, plotted evil, sought to kill, and traveled in packs ten strong?

They hadn't even considered it.

Their party was weak, inexperienced, unfamiliar with combat, had no money nor luck, and most importantly, they were overwhelmingly outnumbered.

It was a common mistake, the kind you hear about all the time.

"Oh!"

Priestess's long sleeves finally got tangled up in her legs, and she fell gracelessly to the ground. Her face and hands received liberal scrapes, but much worse, she lost her grip on Wizard.

Priestess rushed to pull her back up—a girl she hadn't even known a few days before.

"I-I'm sorry! Are you all right?!"

"Ur, hrrg..."

Instead of an answer, blood-flecked spittle bubbled from Wizard's mouth.

Priestess had been so focused on running that she hadn't noticed Wizard beginning to tremble violently. It felt as if Wizard's entire body were on fire, sweat soaking her thick cape.

"Wh-why...?"

Priestess aimed the question directly at herself. Had her prayer not reached the goddess?

Beset by that worry, Priestess used precious time to work off Wizard's outer garments and check the wound.

But the miracle had worked as intended. Wizard's abdomen was blood soaked but smooth. The wound was gone.

"U-uh, i-in times like— In times like this, what should I...?"

Her mind was blank.

She knew a bit of emergency first aid. And she could still use her miracles.

But would another healing miracle really help? Was there something else she should try? For that matter, in her wretched state, could she even focus enough to make an effective petition to the goddess?

"Ahh? Aaahh!"

The moment she'd wasted had been the one that counted. Priestess grew faint as a sudden pain overwhelmed her.

She heard a whistle—something running?—and then her left shoulder lit up with a burning pain. She glanced at it and found an arrow buried deep in her flesh. Blood seeped up and stained her vestments.

Priestess was not wearing any armor. The arrow had ripped savagely through her clothes and into the lovely shoulder beneath. The Precepts forbade excessive armor, and she had no money in any case. Now every tiny movement seemed amplified a hundred times and provoked a heat and pain as though she had been stuck with burning tongs.

"Aaaaghh...!"

All she could do was clench her teeth, keep the tears from her eyes, and stare down the goblins.

Two armed monsters approached. Leering grins split their faces; threads of drool hung from the edges of their mouths.

It would be best if she could bite off her tongue and die. But her goddess did not allow suicide, and she seemed destined to suffer the same fate as her friends.

Would they slice her open? Or rape her? Or both?

"Ohh...no..."

She trembled; her teeth started chattering helplessly.

Priestess pulled Wizard close, using her own body to shield her companion, but suddenly she felt something warm and wet on her legs. The goblins seemed to pick up the scent, and their faces twisted in disgust.

Priestess desperately repeated the name of the Earth Mother, trying to avoid seeing what was in front of her.

There was no hope.

But then...

"Wha...?"

Deep within the darkness, there was a light.

It was like the evening star shining proudly against the encroaching twilight.

A single, ever-so-small but vividly shining point of light, and it steadily came closer.

The light was accompanied by the calm, determined footsteps of someone who held no doubts about where they were going.

The goblins looked back in confusion. Had their friends let some prey slip past?

And then, just behind the goblins, she saw him.

He was not very impressive.

He wore dirty leather armor and a filthy steel helm. On his left arm, a shield was fastened, and in his hand was a torch. His right hand grasped a sword that seemed a strange length. Priestess couldn't help thinking that her own woefully unprepared party had seemed better prepaired than this.

No, she wanted to shout, *stay away!* But terror froze her tongue, and she could not call out. She was deeply humiliated that she lacked Fighter's courage.

The two goblins turned toward the newcomer, demonstrating no reluctance to show their backs to the powerless Priestess. They would deal with her later. One nocked an arrow to his bowstring, drew, and fired.

It was a crude, stone-headed arrow. And the goblin was frankly a terrible archer.

But darkness is the goblin's ally.

No one could dodge an arrow that flew suddenly out of the blackness...

"Hmph."

Even as he offered a derisive snort, the man cut the projectile out of the air with one swift swipe of his sword.

Incapable of comprehending the implication of what had just happened, the second goblin leaped at the man. The creature wielded the only weapon he carried, another of the monsters' rusty daggers. His blade found a chink at the man's shoulder and drove deep.

"Nooo!"

Priestess gave a scream—but there was no other sound. The goblin's blow made only a quiet scrape of metal on metal.

The blade had been stopped by the mail beneath the man's leather armor.

The bewildered goblin pushed harder with his blade. The newcomer made the most of it.

"GAYOU?!" The goblin cried out as the man's shield bashed into him with a thud and pressed him against the stone.

"You first...," the man said coldly.

His meaning became clear when he took his torch and drove it dispassionately into the goblin's face.

An unbearable muffled screech. The stench of burning flesh filled the cave.

The goblin struggled, half mad with pain, but pinned by the shield, he couldn't even claw at his own face.

At last, he stopped moving, his limbs flopping lifelessly to the ground. The man made sure the monster was still, then slowly pulled his shield away.

There was a heavy *whumph* as the goblin tumbled to the ground, its face scorched.

The man gave the monster a casual kick, rolling him over, and then stepped deeper into the cave.

"Next."

It was a bizarre spectacle. Priestess was no longer the only one who was terrified.

The goblin with the bow unconsciously took a step back, understandably looking ready to abandon his companion and flee. *Courage*, after all, is the last word anyone associates with goblins.

But now Priestess was behind it.

She exhaled sharply. And this time, she was able to move. She may have had an arrow in her shoulder, a goblin in front of her, her legs giving out beneath her, and her unconscious companion weighing her down, but she moved.

With her free arm, Priestess thrust her sounding staff at the goblin.

It was a meaningless gesture. She hadn't even really meant to do it, acting on instinct.

But it was more than enough to make the goblin pause for an instant.

In that instant, the creature thought harder about what to do than he ever had in his entire life. But before he could reach a decision, his half-formed answer was slammed into the stone wall, propelled by the sword the armored warrior had thrown through him.

Half of the goblin's head remained on the wall. The other half, with the rest of him, collapsed to the ground.

"That's two."

The brutal fight over, he ground his boot into the slain goblin's cadaver.

He was stained crimson with the monster's blood, from his grimy steel helm and leather armor to the mail made of chain-linked metal rings that covered his entire body.

A small, battered shield was fastened to his left arm, and in one hand, he held a brightly burning torch.

Heel braced against the creature's corpse, he reached down with his free hand and casually withdrew his sword from its skull. It was a cheap-looking blade, its length poorly conceived, and now it was drenched in the goblin's brains.

Lying on the ground, an arrow in her shoulder, the young girl's thin frame shook with fear. Her sweet, classically lovely face framed by long hair almost a translucent gold was scrunched up into a mess of tears and sweat.

Her slim arms, her feet—her whole gorgeous body was clad in the vestments of a priestess. The sounding staff she clutched jangled, the rings hanging on it striking one another in time with the quaking of her hands.

Who was this man before her?

So strange was his appearance, the aura that cloaked him, that she imagined he might be a goblin himself—or perhaps something far worse, something she had no knowledge of yet.

"Wh-who are you...?" she asked, pushing down her terror and pain.

After a pause, the man answered, "Goblin Slayer."

A killer. Not of dragons or vampires, but the lowliest of monsters: goblins.

Normally, the name might have seemed comically simple. But to Priestess, at that moment, it was anything but funny.

§

How must she have looked to the man—Goblin Slayer—as she sat dumbly, forgetting even the pain in her shoulder? He strode closer until he loomed over her, frightening Priestess and making her tremble.

Even now, up close and with the torch illuminating him, his visor hid his face, and she couldn't see his eyes. It was as if the armor was filled with the same darkness as the cave.

"You just registered?" Goblin Slayer asked quietly, noticing the rank tag hanging around her neck. He had one, too. It swayed gently in the light of the torch, which he had set on the floor. The color reflected dimly in that little bubble of light—it was unmistakably silver.

Priestess let out a small "oh…" She knew what that color meant. It was the third-highest rank in the Guild's ten-level system.

Only a few people in history had achieved Platinum rank, and those of Gold rank usually worked for the national government, but after those came Silver, indicating some of the most-skilled unaffiliated adventurers plying their trade independently.

"You're…Silver rank." He was a hardened veteran who could hardly have been further removed from the Porcelain-ranked Priestess.

"I'm sure if you wait a while, some other adventurers will show up…"

Could this have been the adventurer about whom Guild Girl had been speaking?

"So you *can* talk."

"Huh?"

"You're lucky."

Goblin Slayer's hands moved so easily, she didn't have time to react.

"Wha—? Ahh!"

The arrow's hooks tore her flesh as he pulled it out, the sudden wave of pain leaving her breathless. Blood flowed from the wound as her eyes welled up with tears.

With the same casual manner, Goblin Slayer reached for a bag on his belt and took out a small bottle.

"Drink this."

Through the clear glass, she saw a green liquid that emitted gentle phosphorescence—a healing potion.

Just what Priestess and her party had wanted but had had neither money nor time to buy.

She could have simply taken it but instead glanced back and forth between the bottle and the wounded Wizard.

"S-sir!" To her surprise, when she managed to make her voice work once, the words came pouring out of her. "C-couldn't we give it to her? My miracle couldn't—"

"Where is she hurt? What happened?"

"I-it was a dagger…in her stomach…"

"A dagger…"

Goblin Slayer felt Wizard's abdomen in that same assured way. When he jabbed it with a finger, she coughed up more blood. Throughout his brisk examination, he didn't so much as glance at Priestess, who huddled protectively over Wizard. Then he said flatly, "Give up."

Shocked, Priestess turned pale and swallowed heavily. She hugged Wizard tighter.

"Look." Goblin Slayer pulled out the dagger still lodged in the mail under his shoulder. A dark, viscous liquid she couldn't identify was slathered all along the blade.

"Poison."

"P-poison…?"

"They make it from a mixture of their own spittle and excrement, along with herbs they find in the wild."

"You're lucky."

Priestess gulped again as the full meaning of Goblin Slayer's words dawned on her.

Lucky the arrowhead hadn't been dipped in poison, so she was still here. Lucky the goblin with the dagger hadn't been the first to attack her…

"When this poison gets in your system, first you have trouble breathing. Your tongue starts to spasm, then your whole body. Soon, you develop a fever, lose consciousness, then you die."

He wiped the chipped blade with the goblin's loincloth and stashed it on his belt, then murmured inside his helmet, "They're such dirty creatures."

"I-if she's been poisoned, all we need is to cure it, right...?"

"If you mean an antidote, then I have one, but the poison's been in her for too long. It's too late."

"Oh...!"

Just then, Wizard's rolling eyes focused ever so briefly. She gurgled from the blood in her throat, and with trembling lips, she formed words without a sound, without voice. "...ill...e..."

"Understood."

No sooner had he said it than Goblin Slayer cut Wizard's throat.

Wizard jumped, gave a low moan, then coughed up one more mouthful of bloody foam and died.

Inspecting the blade, Goblin Slayer clicked his tongue when he saw it had been blunted by fat.

"Don't be upset," he said.

"How can you say that?!" Priestess exclaimed. "Maybe...maybe we still could have...helped her..." She clutched Wizard's body, gone limp and lifelessly heavy.

But—

She couldn't get the rest of the words out. Had Wizard really been beyond saving? And if so, was killing her a kindness? Priestess did not know.

She only knew she had not yet been given the miracle cure, which neutralized poison. There was an antidote here, but it belonged to the man in front of her. It wasn't hers to give. Priestess sat on the ground shaking, unable to drink the potion or even to stand.

"Listen," Goblin Slayer said brusquely. "These monsters aren't bright, but they're not fools. They were at least smart enough to take out your spell caster first." He paused, then pointed. "Look there."

Hanging from the wall were a dead rat and a crow's feather. "Those are goblin totems. There's a shaman here."

"A shaman...?"

"You don't know about shamans?"

Priestess shook her head uneasily.

"They're spell casters. Better than your friend here."

Goblin spell casters? Priestess had never heard of such a thing. If she had, maybe her party would still be alive…

No.

She resigned herself to the thought in her heart. Even if they had known, they wouldn't have considered these shamans something to be afraid of. Goblins were weak prey, a way for new adventurers to cut their teeth.

Or so she had believed until earlier that day.

"Did you see any big ones?" Goblin Slayer studied her face again as she knelt on the ground.

This time—just barely—she could see his eyes. A cold, almost mechanical light shone from within that dirty helmet.

Priestess stirred and then stiffened, disturbed by the unflinching gaze that watched her from inside the helm. She suddenly remembered the warm moisture on her legs.

She had been attacked by goblins, watched her friends die in moments, saw her party all but annihilated, and she alone had survived.

It seemed unreal.

The throbbing pain in her shoulder and the humiliation of wetting herself, on the other hand, were undeniable.

"Y-yes, there was one…I think…Just running away, took everything I had…" She shook her head weakly, trying to call up the dim memory.

"That was a hobgoblin. Maybe they took on a wanderer as a guard."

"A hob… You mean a hearth fairy?"

"Distant relative."

Goblin Slayer checked his weapons and armor, then stood. "I'll follow their tunnel. I have to deal with them here."

Priestess looked up at him. He was already looking away from her, staring into the blackness ahead.

"Can you make it back on your own, or will you wait here?"

She clung to her sounding staff with exhausted hands, forcing her trembling legs to push her up as tears beaded in her eyes.

"I'm…going…with you!"

It was her only choice. She couldn't bear either going back by herself or being left there all alone.

Goblin Slayer nodded. "Then drink the potion."

As Priestess gulped down the bitter medicine, the heat in her shoulder began to fade. The potion contained at least ten different herbs and wouldn't do anything dramatic, but it would stop the pain.

Priestess gave a relieved sigh. It was the first time she had ever drunk a potion.

Goblin Slayer watched her down the last of it. "All right," he said, and he set off into the murk. There was no hesitation in his stride; he never paused to look back at her. She scurried to keep up with him, afraid of being left behind.

As they went, she cast a glance back. Back at the still, silent Wizard.

There was nothing Priestess could say. Biting her lip, she bowed her head deeper and vowed to come back for her friend.

§

Somehow they didn't encounter any goblins on the short trek to the tunnel. They did, however, find awful chunks of meat scattered about. Perhaps it had once been human. There was no way to know. There was enough blood in the small cavern to choke on, and its smell mixed with the thick odor of scattered viscera.

"Err, eurrggh…"

Priestess spotted the body of Warrior and reflexively fell to her knees and vomited.

It seemed like her last meal of bread and wine had happened years ago. For that matter, it might have been an eon since Warrior had invited her on this adventure.

"Nine…" Goblin Slayer nodded. He had been counting the goblin corpses, unperturbed by the scene around them.

"Judging from the scale of the nest, there's probably less than half left."

He took a sword and dagger from Warrior's body and hung them from his own belt. He checked the goblins' other victims as well but apparently found nothing that satisfied him.

Priestess, wiping her mouth, gave him a reproving look, but he didn't pause.

"How many of you were there?"

"What?"

"Guild Girl only said some amateurs had gone goblin hunting."

"There were four of— Oh!" she accidentally shouted, wiping furiously at her mouth with both hands. "M-my other party member…!" How could she have forgotten?

She didn't see Fighter's body. Fighter, who had sacrificed herself, suffering unspeakable things to save the others, was nowhere to be found.

"A girl?"

"Yes…"

Goblin Slayer held the torch close and carefully searched the floor of the cave. There were fresh footprints, blood, a dirty liquid, and a track like something had been dragged along the ground.

"It looks like they took her deeper in. I can't say if she's alive or not," he said, fingering several long strands of hair to which scraps of skin still clung.

Priestess nearly jumped up. "Then we have to save her—"

But Goblin Slayer didn't answer. He lit a new torch, then tossed the old one into a side tunnel. "Goblins have excellent night vision. Keep it lit. The dark is our enemy… Listen."

She obeyed, straining her ears for any sound.

From the blackness beyond the flame of the torch, there were footsteps, *slap-slap-slap.*

A goblin! Probably coming to investigate the light from the torch.

Goblin Slayer took one of the daggers from his belt and flung it into the darkness.

There was a harsh sound as it pierced something. The body of a goblin rolled into the dim torchlight. The moment he saw it, Goblin Slayer leaped forward and drove his sword through the creature's heart. The goblin died without a sound, for the dagger had run through its throat. The whole thing happened almost too quickly to track.

"Ten."

As Goblin Slayer added to his count, Priestess peered into the tunnel and asked timidly, "Can you see in the dark, too?"

"Hardly."

Goblin Slayer didn't bother retrieving the fat-dulled blade from the body. Instead, he took up the sword Warrior had carried, clicking his tongue as he saw it was too long for the narrow tunnels.

Next he picked up a spear from the goblin he had just killed. It was roughly hewn from animal bone, but a spear for a goblin is only a bit longer than a knife for a full-grown man.

"It's just practice. I know exactly where their necks are."

"Practice? How much practice…?"

"A lot."

"A lot?"

"You're just full of questions, aren't you?"

Priestess was silent. She hung her head in embarrassment.

"What can you use?"

"I'm sorry?" She hurriedly raised her head again, not understanding what he meant.

Goblin Slayer never let his attention waver from the tunnel as he spoke. "Which miracles?"

"I have Minor Heal and Holy Light, sir."

"How many uses?"

"Three in all. I…I have two left." It was nothing extraordinary, but Priestess was one of the more accomplished beginners. It was an achievement simply to be able to pray to the goddess, make a petition, and be granted a miracle in the first place. And then, not many people could bear to join their soul with the goddess repeatedly. That took experience.

"That's considerably more than I expected," he said. This was praise, she supposed, but she had trouble feeling like it. His tone was dutiful and cool, hardly revealing any emotion.

"Holy Light, then. Minor Heal won't do us any good here. Don't waste your miracles on it."

"Y-yes, sir…"

"That was a scout we killed. We've got the right tunnel."

With the tip of the spear, he pointed deeper into the hole from which the goblin had come. "But their scout won't return. Neither will the ones who killed your party. I finished them off."

Priestess was silent.

"What would you do?"

"What?"

"If you were a goblin. What would you do?"

At the unexpected question, Priestess tapped a slender finger against her chin, thinking furiously. What would she do if she were a goblin?

Her hand, which had once assisted with services at the Temple, seemed too white to be an adventurer's.

"...Set an ambush?"

"Exactly," Goblin Slayer said in his calm voice. "And we're going to walk right into it. Get ready."

Priestess paled but nodded.

Goblin Slayer took out a coil of rope and some wooden stakes and laid them at his feet.

"I have a mantra for you," he said, not taking his eyes off his work. "Remember it. The words are *tunnel entrance*. You forget them, you die."

"Y-yes, sir!" Priestess clasped her sounding staff with both hands.

Tunnel entrance, tunnel entrance, she repeated desperately to herself.

The only thing she could rely on was this mysterious man who called himself Goblin Slayer. If he abandoned her, then she and Fighter and the kidnapped village girls were all lost.

A moment later, Goblin Slayer finished his preparations. "Let's go."

Priestess followed him as quickly as she could, past the rope and into the tunnel.

The tunnel was remarkably sturdy, not something that seemed to have been built just for mounting surprise attacks. With every step, dirt fell from tree roots that had pushed through the ceiling, but there didn't seem to be any danger of collapse. The gradual downward slope made Priestess uneasy, however. Humans didn't belong here.

She should have seen it from the start, and now that she had realized, it was too late: *Goblins spend their whole lives underground.* True, they were nothing like dwarves, but why had she and the others underestimated the goblins so badly just because they weren't physically strong?

Well, it's too late for regrets...

Priestess stepped carefully by the faint light of the torch. She glanced up at Goblin Slayer's back. His movements betrayed neither hesitation nor fear. Did he know what lay ahead?

"We're almost there." He stopped so suddenly, Priestess nearly ran into him. She straightened up quicker than he could turn to look back with his mechanical movements.

"Now, Holy Light."

"Y-yes, sir. I'm ready…when you are."

She took a deep breath and let it out. Then she held her staff firmly in place. Goblin Slayer likewise adjusted his grip on his torch and spear.

"Do it."

"O Earth Mother, abounding in mercy, grant your sacred light to we who are lost in darkness…"

Goblin Slayer leaped forward as Priestess raised her staff toward the blackness. Its tip began shining with an illumination that became as brilliant as the sun. A miracle of the Earth Mother.

With the light at his back, Goblin Slayer flew headlong into the monsters' hall.

Perhaps they had simply appropriated the largest cavern in the cave complex. The goblins waiting in the shoddily constructed room came into view.

"GAUI?"

"GORRR?"

There were six goblins there, as well as one big one and one seated on a chair wearing a skull on his head. The monsters squinted against the sudden, pure light and howled in confusion.

Also there, lying motionless, were several young women.

Some bleak thing had no doubt been happening in that room.

"Six goblins, one hob, one shaman, eight total." Goblin Slayer counted his opponents without so much as a tremor in his voice.

Of course, not all the goblins were clenching their eyes shut and keening.

"OGAGO, GAROA…" The shaman seated on the throne waved his staff and recited an unintelligible spell.

"GUAI?" He was interrupted by Goblin Slayer's spear skewering him through the torso. He gave a death rattle and tumbled backward off his chair.

The goblins stood transfixed by this tragedy, and Goblin Slayer seized the moment. Warrior's sword rang as Goblin Slayer freed it from its scabbard.

"All right, let's get out of here."

"What?! Y-yes, sir!"

Even as he spoke, Goblin Slayer was already turning and dashing off. Shocked at his speed and at a loss about what to do, Priestess followed him. The goblins recovered their wits as the light receded and soon gave chase.

In the space of a breath, Goblin Slayer was far ahead of Priestess as she ran up the slope. Was he used to taking the role of vanguard and rear guard, or was this the result of sheer training and experience? Whatever the case, it was incredible to her that he could be so nimble while clad in leather armor and mail, his vision limited by his helmet.

It was when she saw him jump lightly at the mouth of the tunnel that the words of his mantra came rushing back to her. "Oh no—!" She barely missed the trip wire on the ground. Goblin Slayer was already pressed up against the wall, and Priestess hurried to do the same against the opposite side.

"GUIII!!"

"GYAA!!"

They could hear the enraged voices and pounding footfalls of the goblins coming up the slope. Priestess took a furtive peek and saw a hulking shape at the front of the pack—the hobgoblin.

"Now! Do it again!" Goblin Slayer flung the words at her.

Priestess gave a nod and thrust her staff with its symbols of her priesthood toward the tunnel. She spoke the words of the prayer without a stutter.

"O Earth Mother, abounding in mercy, grant your sacred light to we who are lost in darkness…"

Merciful the Earth Mother's light was to them, but not to the eyes of the goblins, which burned at its brilliance.

"GAAU?!"

The blinded hobgoblin stumbled on the trip wire and took an ungainly fall.

"Eleven." Goblin Slayer vaulted in and ruthlessly thrust his sword into the creature's brain. It gurgled once, twice, then spasmed and died.

"H-here come the others!" Priestess called. She was out of miracles, and the repeated soul-effacing ritual had left her enervated, her face bloodless from exertion.

"I know." Goblin Slayer whipped a bottle from his bag and threw it against the hobgoblin's body. It shattered, releasing a thick black substance from inside. The cloying smell made Priestess think perhaps it was some unfamiliar poison.

"See you in hell."

Goblin Slayer kicked the drenched body into the tunnel. The oncoming goblins, caught off guard by the hunk of meat rolling toward them, slammed their swords into it.

It was an instinctive reaction. When they realized it was their guardian they had stabbed, they panicked. The goblins struggled to extract the weapons, buried deep in the hobgoblin's flesh and now covered in the black substance...

"Twelve, thirteen."

They were too late.

Without a hint of remorse, Goblin Slayer threw the torch into the tunnel with them. There was a *whoosh* as the hobgoblin's corpse went up in flames, taking their two pursuers with it.

"GYUIAAAAAA!!" The screeching goblins flailed on the ground, burning as they rolled all the way back to the bottom of the slope. Priestess choked on the smell of roasting meat that floated up to her.

"Wh-what was that?"

"Some call it Medea's Oil. Others, petroleum. It's gasoline." He had gotten it from an alchemist, he said nonchalantly, adding, "Awfully expensive for such a simple effect."

"B-but inside—in there, the kidnapped girls—"

"The fire won't spread far with just a few bodies to feed on. If those girls are still alive, this isn't going to kill them." He muttered, "And we're not out of goblins yet," causing Priestess to bite her lip again.

"A-are you going back in, then?"

"No. When they can't breathe anymore, they'll come out on their own."

Goblin Slayer's sword was lost now, stuck in a burning hobgoblin corpse at the bottom of a tunnel. He probably wasn't eager to fight with a brain-soaked blade, anyway.

He picked up the weapon the hobgoblin had dropped, a stone ax. It was just a rock tied to a stick—rough in every sense of the word. But then, that made it easy to use, too.

Goblin Slayer swung the ax rapidly through the air, testing it, and found he could wield it easily with one hand.

Satisfied, he reached into his bag and pulled out another torch.

"Here," Priestess said, offering a flint, but Goblin Slayer hardly looked at her.

"These beasts never think somebody might set an ambush for *them*," he said.

She was silent.

"Don't worry." He swung the ax in carefully coordinated strokes, landing each blow on the flint. "It'll be over soon."

He was right.

He dealt with each of the goblins as they emerged from the flames and smoke. One tripped on the rope and found his head split open. The second hopped over the rope but was laid low by the waiting ax. The third was the same. The ax wouldn't come out of the cheekbone of the fourth creature, so Goblin Slayer took the monster's club instead.

"That's seventeen. We're going in."

"Y-yes, sir!" Priestess rushed to keep up with Goblin Slayer as he dove into the roiling smoke.

The hall was a terrible sight. The hobgoblin was burned beyond recognition, its companions little better. The shaman lay with the spear still through its body. And the girls were lying in filth on the floor.

As Goblin Slayer had predicted, the smoke floated above them.

But to survive is not always a blessing—something Priestess realized when she picked out Fighter's body among them.

"Uggh…euhrrrgh…"

Nothing was left in Priestess's stomach. She brought up only bile, bitter and burning in her throat, and she felt tears welling in her eyes again.

"Well, then."

While Priestess was vomiting, Goblin Slayer had stamped out the flames running along the gasoline on the floor.

He strode over to the speared shaman. The goblin looked surprised by its own death. It lay completely still. The image of Goblin Slayer standing over him was reflected in his glassy eyes.

"I thought so," Goblin Slayer said, immediately raising his club.

"GUI?!" As the startled shaman jumped up, the club came down, and then he was dead for good.

Shaking the spattered brains off the club, Goblin Slayer muttered, "Eighteen. The high-level ones are tough."

Goblin Slayer began to kick violently at the throne, now vacant in every sense. Priestess heaved again as she saw it was made of human bones.

"Typical goblin trick. Look."

"Wh...what?" Priestess wiped her eyes and mouth as she raised her head. Behind the throne hung one of the rotten wooden boards the goblins used in place of doors.

A hidden store—or was that all it was? Priestess gripped her staff at a clattering sound from within.

"You were lucky."

As Goblin Slayer pulled the board aside, there were several high-pitched screams. Along with a stash of plunder, four terrified goblin children crouched inside.

"These creatures multiply quickly. If your party had come any later, there would've been fifty of them, and they would have attacked en masse."

At the thought of it—of what would have happened to her and everyone—Priestess shivered. She imagined dozens of goblins taking her, bearing half-breed goblin children...

Looking down at the cowering forms, Goblin Slayer adjusted his grip on the club.

"You'll...kill the children, too?" she asked, but she already knew the answer. She quailed as she heard the flat tone of her own voice. Had her heart, her emotions, been numbed by the onslaught of reality? She wanted it to be true. Just this once.

"Of course I will," he said with a calm nod.

He must have seen this before many, many times.

She knew he called himself "Goblin Slayer" for a reason.

"We've destroyed their nest. They'll never forget that, let alone forgive it. And the survivors of a nest learn, become smarter." As he spoke, he casually raised the club, still covered in the shaman's brains. "There is no reason to let them live."

"Even if there was…a good goblin?"

"A good goblin?" He exhaled in a way that suggested he was truly mystified by the idea.

"There might be…if we looked, but…"

He said nothing for a long moment. Then he spoke.

"The only good goblins are the ones that never come out of their holes."

He took a step.

"This will make twenty-two."

§

It's a common story, one heard all the time.

A village is attacked by goblins. Some maidens are kidnapped.

Some rookies decide they're going to get rid of these goblins for their first quest.

But the goblins are too much, and the whole party is slaughtered.

Or maybe just one makes it out and saves the girls, too.

During their captivity, the girls had been forced to serve as the goblins' playthings.

In despair, they take shelter at the Temple.

The lone survivor slowly slips away from the world and never leaves home again.

In this world, these sorts of things are an everyday occurrence, as common as the sunrise.

Or are they? Priestess wasn't sure. Do these life-shattering events really happen all the time?

And if they do, could she, knowing them firsthand, go on believing in the Earth Mother?

In the end, there were only two things of which she was certain.

That she would continue as an adventurer.

And that Goblin Slayer had exterminated every goblin in that nest.

But then, that, too, is no more than another often-told tale.

Somewhere not here. In a place immensely far away yet incredibly close.

Rattle, rattle, a certain deity is rolling dice.

She looks like a sweet little girl, and her name is Illusion.

Again and again she rolls. She's had a pretty good day, and a smile plays on her lips.

But dice pay no heed to the will of the gods.

With a cute little gasp, Illusion hides her face.

Oh! What a terrible roll. She can't even look at it.

But however pretty or sweet she may be, not even Illusion can change numbers on dice.

No equipment and no strategy will help.

Call it chance or fate, these things will happen.

Illusion slumps in disappointment, and one god points and laughs at her.

His name is Truth. *I told you*, he says, so transported with mirth that he claps his hands.

Truth, after all, is without restraint. Cruel.

He tells her she was a fool to gamble on a quest so rich with risks.

Illusion grumbles to herself, but there is nothing she can do.

She herself does not hold back when she takes on fate-guided adventurers.

So how can she complain when her own adventurers happen to die?

It is simply how things work.

Hearing this, some would object to what seems like gods using humans as playthings.

Yet what path is not influenced by chance or fate?

When all your adventurers are dead, though, there is nothing left to do.

It is unfortunate, but this adventure is over.

Ready some new adventurers and try again.

It'll be fine this time. Surely these new ones will—

At that moment, the two deities notice a new adventurer has appeared upon the board.

Truth gives a disgusted grunt.

Illusion gives a delicate start.

He has come.

CHAPTER 2

Cow Girl's Day

She had a familiar dream.

She dreamed of a summer day when she was still small. Eight years old maybe. She had come by herself to her uncle's farm to help deliver a calf. At her tender age, she didn't realize it was just an excuse to let her play.

She was going to help with a birth. That was an important job.

And even better, she was going to get out of the village and go to the city—all by herself!

Of course, she bragged about it to him. She remembered the sulky look that came over his face. He was two years older than her, but he knew nothing of life outside the village. He could hardly imagine a city, let alone the Capital.

True, she was just like him in that respect, but still…

She could no longer remember what started it.

He got angry, they fought, and both ended up in tears. Looking back on it, she thought perhaps she had gone too far, believing she could say whatever she wanted because he was a boy.

Saying too much, hurting him enough that he got really angry. She hadn't considered that might happen. She was young, after all.

Eventually his older sister came to get him and took him home, leading him by the hand.

The truth was, she had wanted to invite him to go with her.

On the carriage to the next town, she looked back at her village out the window's curtain.

Her mother and father had come to see her off. *He* was nowhere to be seen as she waved good-bye to her parents.

As she drifted off in the rumbling carriage, she felt a twinge of regret. She didn't get a chance to apologize.

When she got back, she would have to make up with him…

§

Cow Girl's day started early.

That was because *he* woke up early, even before the rooster crowed dawn.

The first thing he did on waking was to make a lap of the farm. He never neglected this.

When she asked him about it once, he told her he was looking for footprints. "Goblins move at night," he'd said. "They go back to their nests by first light, but they always reconnoiter before an attack." So, he told her, he was checking for footprints, to make sure he didn't miss a sign of goblins.

When he had finished his first inspection, he made another. This time, he was looking for any damage to the fence. And if he found any, he would take it upon himself to get some stakes and planks and repair it.

Cow Girl woke to the sound of his footsteps going past her window. The cock finally began its morning call.

Hearing that casual, self-possessed walk, she slid her naked body off her straw bed, gave a great stretch and a yawn. Then she pulled some underwear over her voluptuous form before opening the window.

The cool, bracing morning wind blew in.

"Good morning! Up early as always, I see!" Cow Girl rested her vast bosom on the window frame and leaned out, calling to his back as he looked at the fence.

"Yeah," he said, turning.

He wore dirty armor, leather plate, and a steel helmet; a shield was fastened to his left arm and a sword hung at his waist.

Just like he always looked. Squinting toward the sun, Cow Girl said, "Good weather today. Mr. Sun is so bright!"

"He is."

"Is Uncle up?"

"No idea."

"Hmm. Well, I'm sure he'll be awake soon."

"Think so?"

"You must be hungry. Let's have breakfast. I'll have it ready in a moment."

"All right."

He nodded slowly.

He's still a man of few words, Cow Girl thought with a smile.

He wasn't like that when they were small. At least, he shouldn't have been.

Only the details of the weather changing, they had the same conversation every morning.

But he was an adventurer, and going on adventures was a risky business. If she was talking to him in the morning, it meant he had survived another day, so she wouldn't object no matter how few words they shared.

Still smiling, Cow Girl squeezed herself into her work clothes and headed lightly toward the kitchen.

They were supposed to take turns preparing meals, but it was Cow Girl who did the actual cooking. In all the years they had lived together, he had hardly ever cooked.

Twice, three times maybe? When I had that cold, I'm sure…

She hadn't told him the soup he'd made was thin and watery for fear he would get upset.

She did think sometimes that since he got up early anyway, maybe he could make breakfast once in a while. But adventurers led unpredictable lives. There was nothing he could do, so she didn't nag him about it.

"Morning, Uncle! Breakfast soon, okay?"

"Yes, morning. Smells good today. My stomach's rumbling." Her uncle, the farm's owner, woke up just as *he* came in from his inspection.

"Good morning, sir."

"Mm-hm…morning." Her uncle replied with a short word and a curt nod to his dutiful greeting.

©Noboru Kannatuki

On the table were cheese, bread, and a creamy soup, all made right there on the farm.

He pushed food into the opening of his visor. Cow Girl watched him delightedly.

"Here's for this month," he said, as if suddenly remembering something. He produced a leather pouch from the bag at his hip and placed it on the table. It made a heavy sound as he set it down, and through its open mouth, gold coins glittered.

"…"

Her uncle looked at it silently, as if reluctant to take it.

One could hardly blame him. The armored man didn't need to be renting space in the stables on some Podunk farm. He could have been staying in the Royal Suite somewhere.

Finally, her uncle gave a small sigh of surrender and drew the pouch toward him.

"Awfully profitable being an adventurer."

"Business has been good lately."

"Is that right? Say, you… Are you…?" Her uncle was normally so good with people, but around this man, he always got tongue-tied. Cow Girl just couldn't understand it…

With a mixture of fear and resignation, her uncle finally continued:

"…Are you going again today?"

"Yes, sir," he answered calmly. Always with that same slow nod. "I'll go to the Guild. Too much work not to."

"I see." Her uncle paused. "Don't get carried away, now."

"No, sir."

Her uncle seemed nonplussed by the man's even voice as he took a sip of warm milk from his glass.

Their morning chats always ended this way. Cow Girl tried to lighten the mood by saying, with forced cheerfulness, "Well, I've got to make some deliveries, so we can go together!"

"Fine." He nodded, but at this, her uncle's expression turned even sterner.

"…I mean, in that case, I can take out the cart," the adventurer quickly amended.

"Oh, Uncle's just a mother hen," Cow Girl said. "I'll be *fine*. I'm a lot stronger than I look, you know!" She rolled up a sleeve and flexed a bicep for his edification.

True enough, her arms were larger than a city girl's her age, but she was not what you would call muscular.

"All right." That was all he said as he finished his breakfast. He left the table without even thanking her for the meal.

"H-hey, wait a minute, slow down!" she said. "I have to get ready, too! Hold on!"

But that, too, was how things always went. Cow Girl wolfed down the rest of her breakfast in a most unladylike way.

She washed down the immense meal—which she needed because of all the work she did—with milk and then took all their dishes to the sink.

"All right, Uncle, we're off!"

"Come back soon. And safely. Please."

"It'll be fine, Uncle. We'll be together."

Still seated at the table, her uncle wore a despondent look, as if to say, *That's what I'm worried about.* Cow Girl's uncle was a kind, good-hearted farmer, as she herself well knew. He just didn't seem to get along with the adventurer. Or rather…her uncle seemed scared of him. Even though there was nothing to be scared of…

…She was pretty sure.

When she got outside, he was already walking down the road beyond the fence. She went to where the cart was kept behind the house, hurriedly but not rushing.

She had loaded the produce the day before, so she had only to pick up the handlebar and push off. As the wheels creaked along, the produce and wine rattled from atop the cart.

He strode along the tree-lined road to town, Cow Girl following behind him, pulling the cart. Each time the load jostled over the gravel, her chest bounced right along with it.

This work was nowhere near difficult enough to be exhausting, but as they went along, she began to sweat a little and breathe a bit harder.

"……"

Suddenly, without a word, he slackened his pace. He didn't stop, of course, but slowed. At the same time, Cow Girl, in a burst of energy, sped up until she was walking at his side.

"Thanks."

"…Not at all." He shook his head as he spared the few words. Perhaps it was his helmet that made the gesture look strangely broad.

"Switch?"

"Nah, I'm all right."

"I see."

The Adventurers Guild also housed an inn and tavern, and that was where Cow Girl would deliver the produce—that was her job. It was where he would go to get the day's quest—that was his job.

She couldn't assist him with his work, so she felt bad somehow getting his help with hers.

"How's it been going?" she asked over the rumble of the cart, glancing sideways at him.

Not that there was much to see. He wore his helmet from the moment he got up every day. Whatever expression he wore, she couldn't see it.

"More goblins lately."

His answers were always short. Short and yet somehow enough. Cow Girl nodded brightly.

"Really?"

"More than usual."

"So you're busy?"

"I am."

"Yeah, you're out all the time these days."

"I am."

"It's great to have plenty of work, huh?"

"No," he said, quietly shaking his head. "It isn't."

"Why not?" she asked, and he replied:

"I would rather have no goblins."

"Yeah…," she said, nodding.

Things would be better with no goblins at all.

§

The road gradually got better, and they could just make out the buildings on the horizon as the bustle of the city drifted to their ears. Here, as in most towns, the Guild Hall was immediately inside the gate. It was also the biggest building in town, towering over its surroundings, even larger than the Earth Mother Temple with its attached infirmary. Ostensibly, this was because so many people from out of town came for the Guild Hall and would need to find it easily.

Cow Girl, for one, was glad it was easy to find.

The Guild also claimed they wanted to be able to quickly apprehend any ne'er-do-wells who were going around calling themselves adventurers.

Then again, it was hard to tell most adventurers from common thugs at a glance.

She took in all the varieties of outrageous armor worn by the people walking the streets and *him* with his steel helm, even though they were in the middle of town, and gave a wry smile.

"Hang on, okay? I'm just gonna drop off the delivery."

"Sure."

Cow Girl quickly left the produce at the service entrance in the back of the building, then exhaled as she wiped the sweat from her forehead. She rang the bell to summon the cook, showed him a tally sheet to confirm she had brought everything as requested, and took his signature. Now all she needed was Guild Girl's signature, and her delivery would be finished.

"Sorry to keep you waiting."

"Not at all."

He was still there when she came out front again, as she'd known he would be.

As they passed through the swinging door of the Guild Hall together, the momentary relief from the sun was swept away by the collective body heat of all the people packed into the building. The Guild Hall was lively as ever.

"I'm gonna go get that signature."

"Sure."

Outside he had waited for her, but inside they would part ways.

He headed for a row of seats along the wall and settled down in one with authority, as though it was reserved for him. Cow Girl waved lightly to him, then headed for the front desk, where a line of visitors waited. There were adventurers, people filing quests, and hangers-on of every sort. Tradesmen from smiths to pawnbrokers, from merchants to medicine hawkers. It occurred to her that adventuring had more expenses than it seemed.

"So, hey. This troll comes at me, right? But I'm like, *Not today!* and I slip past him by *this* much!"

"Oh my, that sounds very tiring. Maybe you should try a Stamina potion."

Cow Girl saw a spear-wielding adventurer eagerly relating his exploits to the girl at the front desk. His impressively slim body, which seemed composed of almost solid muscle, spoke of his strength. The tag around his neck showed he was a Silver-ranked adventurer.

Cow Girl knew this was the third-highest rank in the Guild hierarchy. She knew because it was *his* rank, too.

"Stamina potion? Who needs it? Babe, I just faced down a *troll* with nothing but my spear in my hands. What do you think of that?"

"Oh, I've heard how fearsome trolls are..." As she began feeling troubled, reaching for words, Guild Girl's eyes happened upon *him* sitting by the wall.

"Oh!" Her face instantly brightened.

"Ugh. Goblin Slayer." Spearman gave a cluck as he followed Guild Girl's gaze.

Maybe he had spoken a bit too loudly. The hubbub in the Guild Hall rose as first one visitor, then another looked in *his* direction.

"I can't believe he's Silver rank, too." An elegant knight was shaking her head in disgust. The scars on her platinum armor bespoke many battles and made her all the more striking. "Who knows if he can even fight anything bigger than a goblin? A 'specialist'? Heh! They'll give a Silver rank to anyone these days!"

"Let him be. He never has anything to do with the rest of us, anyway. Who cares what he does?"

A great tank of a warrior gave Knight a dismissive wave of his hand. Was it foolishness or bravery that let him seem so comfortable in his villainous-looking armor? Both he and Knight wore silver tags, so they were no fresh-faced questers, either.

Two boys, though, stood talking in thin leather plate. Each had a dagger, a staff, and a robe.

"Look at him!" one said. "I've never seen armor that dirty!"

"Yeah, the two of us have better stuff than him…"

Their equipment was every bit as cheap as his, but "better" in that there wasn't a scratch on it.

"Stop it," a female paladin about the boys' age said reproachfully. "What if he hears you? I'm sure he's a rookie just like us." The ridicule in their voices was tinged with relief at finding someone else as pathetic as they were. They showed no sign of noticing the silver tag around his neck.

"Heh-heh-heh…" A spell caster in a pointy hat and a scandalous robe seemed to be enjoying the exchange. She was called a witch and was a Silver-ranked magic user. She hugged her staff seductively and hung back near the wall aloofly from the goings-on.

The whispering spread throughout the room. Those who knew him and those who didn't, all murmuring together.

And in the middle of it all, *he* sat quietly in his seat as though oblivious.

He doesn't care. He's not acting—he really doesn't care. So I guess there's no point in getting angry for him…

Cow Girl held her tongue, but she wasn't happy.

At that moment, a frown still fixed on her face, she happened to meet Guild Girl's eyes. Behind her perpetual smile, she had the same look as Cow Girl.

Resignation. Anger. Disgust. And…the recognition that there was nothing she could do.

I know how you feel.

Guild Girl closed her eyes for a second and sighed.

"Excuse me, please. I'll be right back."

"Yes, er, ahem, please do… I'll be waiting. I haven't finished telling you about my brave exploits—er, making my report yet!"

"Yes, I understand." Guild Girl disappeared into a back office.

A moment later, she poked her head into the hall. She held a heavy-looking stack of papers with both arms. With many a huff and puff, she brought them over to the corkboard on the wall.

"All right, everyone! It's time to post the morning quests!" Guild Girl's voice carried across the hall, silencing the murmurs in the room. Her braids bounced merrily as she waved to get the crowd's attention.

"Finally!" Eyes sparkling, the adventurers thronged Guild Girl, knocking over chairs in their haste. After all, if they didn't take on a quest, they wouldn't eat today. Such was the life of an adventurer. The nature as well as the proffered reward of the quest would influence the adventurers' reputations. And how much good they contributed to the world—a value common folk referred to simply as "experience points"—would determine their rank. And everyone wanted to move up in rank.

An adventurer's rank would earn him trust, after all. No one would entrust an important quest to a Porcelain or Obsidian adventurer, no matter how skilled they were.

With Guild Girl looking on, the gathered adventurers squabbled as they pulled quests from the board.

"Porcelain-ranked stuff is so…cheap. I don't want to spend my whole life chasing rats out of the sewers."

"Well, not much we can do. Hey, how about this one?"

"Goblin slaying? Nice. Indeed, sounds like a job for some beginners."

"Oooh, that's a good one. I want to kill some goblins…"

"No! You heard Guild Girl—we need to start with the sewers!"

"How about dragons? Any dragons? Something martial!"

"Oh, give it up, you haven't got the gear for it. Stick to rounding up bandits. The pay's not bad."

"Hey, I was looking at that quest!"

"Well, I got it first. Guess you'll have to find another one."

Spearman from earlier was late to the fray, and he found himself pushed back by the crowd until he fell flat on his butt. He jumped up and flew back into the fracas with a roar.

"Okay, everyone, there's no need to fight," Guild Girl said placatingly, the smile still pasted on her face.

"Hmph." At length, Cow Girl wandered away from Guild Girl. She didn't want to get caught up in this, and it didn't look like she would be able to get that signature anytime soon.

Bored, Cow Girl let her gaze drift toward the wall. *He* was still sitting there.

She had once said, "We'd better hurry or all the work will be gone," but he had replied, "Goblin slaying isn't popular." Farmers posted the jobs, so the rewards were meager, and as they were seen as low-level quests, the more experienced adventurers wouldn't take them.

So he waited for the reception area to clear out. There was no hurry.

And…he never said it, but Cow Girl thought he was waiting so new adventurers could have their pick of the quests first. Not that she would suggest this to him. He would just say, *"Is that so?"* like he always did.

"Hmm…" If she was going to be stuck here anyway, maybe she should go wait with him?

She shouldn't have hesitated.

"Ah…" Someone else approached him before she could.

A young female adventurer. She wore priestess vestments over her delicate frame, the symbol of the Earth Mother hanging from her sounding staff.

"…Hi," she said shortly, standing in front of him. She looked uncomfortable as she gave a small bow.

"Yeah." That was all he said. Whatever he might be thinking was hidden inside that helmet. He didn't seem to notice Priestess was even more flustered by her inability to elicit a proper response from him.

"I bought some equipment. Just like you told me." She rolled up the sleeves of her vestments. A set of brand-new mail clung to her slender body, the chained links glimmering faintly.

"Not bad."

Someone who didn't know any better might take the scene the wrong way, but his words held no hint of innuendo.

He finally turned toward Priestess, looked her up and down, and nodded.

"The rings are a bit wide, but it will be enough to stop their blades."

"Mother Superior was very displeased with me. She wanted to know what servant of the Earth Mother would wear armor."

"She probably doesn't know much about goblins."

"It's not that. It's a violation of the Precepts…"

"If it will interfere with your miracles, maybe you should switch faiths."

"My prayers will reach the Earth Mother!"

"Then there's no problem."

Priestess puffed out her cheeks angrily. Both of them were silent for a moment.

"Not going to sit?"

"Oh, I-I will! I will sit!"

Blushing, she hurriedly lowered herself into the chair next to him. Her little behind made a cute *buhmp* as she sat down.

Priestess laid her staff across her knees and clasped her hands, as if trying to shrink into the seat. Apparently, she was quite nervous.

"Hmph." Cow Girl let out an unconscious grunt, but it wasn't as though he had never mentioned this girl. She was an adventurer he had been partied with for about a month now. He didn't actually say that he had found her on her first adventure and taken her under his wing—but Cow Girl had put this together from the bits and pieces she got out of him.

On the one hand, she had always been worried about him out there by himself, so she was glad there was someone with him now. On the other hand...did she have to be so *young*?

Cow Girl came with him to the Guild Hall every day, but this was the first time she had seen Priestess in person. She was so slim she looked like a strong hug would break her in half. Cow Girl looked down at her own ample body and gave a little sigh.

Priestess never noticed Cow Girl watching her. Instead, still blushing furiously but seeming to have worked up her courage, she opened her mouth.

"A-about the other day..."

The high pitch and quick pace of her words must have been due to nerves, surely.

"I-I think destroying the whole cave with that fire mixture was too...too much!"

"Why is that?" He continued to sound as if none of this surprised him. "We can hardly leave the goblins to themselves there."

"Y-yes, but what...what about the consequences? What if the whole m-mountain came down?"

"I'm more worried about goblins."

"I know! I-I'm trying to tell you that shortsightedness is the problem!"

"...I see."

"A-and another thing! I think the way you get rid of...of the smell should be a little...a little more...!" She started leaning off her seat as she talked.

His tone suggested he was growing annoyed. "So, have you learned the times to attack?" Priestess swallowed, caught off guard by the sudden change of subject.

Cow Girl, innocently eavesdropping, giggled to herself.

He hasn't changed a bit since we were young.

"It's…early in the morning or in the evening," Priestess answered, while trying to show with her face that she wasn't letting him off that easily.

"Why?"

"B-because those are evening and morning for goblins, respectively."

"Correct. High noon is midnight for them. Their guard is tightest then. Next question: How do you attack a nest?"

"Well…if possible, you build a fire to smoke them out. Because it's…it's dangerous…inside the nest."

"Right. Only enter when you have no time or no other choice. Or when you want to be sure you've killed every last one of them."

He interrogated her as she struggled to come up with answers. "Items?"

"M-mainly potions and torches."

"Is that all?"

"A-and rope. There's always a use for rope…I guess."

"Don't forget it. Spells and miracles."

"Y-your items can often substitute for spells and miracles, so you should save your magic for when you need it."

"Weapons."

"Um, you should have…"

"No, you shouldn't. Take them from the enemy. They have swords, spears, axes, clubs, bows. I don't need any special tools. I'm a warrior."

"…Yes, sir." She nodded like a child who had been scolded by her teacher.

"Change your weapons, change your tactics. Doing the same thing over and over is a good way to get yourself killed."

"Um, may I…write this down?"

"No. If they took the notes from you, they'd learn from them. You have to know everything by heart." He spoke calmly while Priestess labored to commit his words to memory. It truly seemed like the back-and-forth between teacher and pupil.

Did he ever talk this much? Cow Girl shifted uneasily as the question rose in her mind.

She couldn't understand why it left her so restless. She wanted to get that signature as soon as she could and go home.

"All right," he said, standing suddenly. Looking around, she realized the crowd of adventurers was just shuffling off to their business. There was much to do—prepare equipment, stock up on food and supplies, gather information.

Priestess hurried to keep up with him as he strode toward Guild Girl with hardly a glance at the departing questers.

"Ah..." Cow Girl had missed her chance again. Her voice, like her outstretched hand, hung in the air.

"Oh, Mr. Goblin Slayer! Good morning! How nice to see you again today!" Guild Girl's voice and face carried all the brightness that Cow Girl's lacked.

"Any goblins?"

"Why, yes! Not too many today, I'm afraid, but there are three quests involving goblins." As he stood there calmly, Guild Girl picked out some papers with a practiced hand. She seemed to have prepared them in advance.

"The village by the western mountains has a medium-sized nest. The village by the northern river has a small nest. And there's a small nest in the southern woods."

"Villages again?"

"Yes. They're all farmers, as usual. I wonder if the goblins are targeting them."

"Maybe." He had taken her joking words in dead earnest. "Has anyone else taken on any of these quests?"

"Yes. A group of rookies are in the southern woods. That one is a request from a village near the forest."

"Beginners," he murmured. "Who was in their party?"

"Let's see...," Guild Girl said. She licked her thumb and began paging through a sheaf of papers.

"One warrior, one wizard, and one paladin. All Porcelain rank."

"Hmm. That's fairly well-balanced."

"They were here earlier... Just three people? They'll never survive!"

Priestess's panicked squeak contrasted sharply with his measured assessment. "I mean, we had four, and…"

She went pale and trembled slightly. She gripped her sounding staff tightly.

Cow Girl looked away, the uneasy feeling growing sharper within her.

Why hadn't she realized it sooner?

He meets an adventurer on her first quest…an adventurer…

She should have understood what that meant.

"I tried to explain to them…I really did. But they insisted they'd be fine," Guild Girl said uncomfortably. She obviously knew Priestess's story.

But at the end of the day, adventurers were responsible for themselves.

Priestess looked up at him imploringly.

"We can't leave them! If we don't help them…"

His answer was immediate. "Go if you want."

"What…?"

"I'm taking out the mountain nest. At the very least, a hob or a shaman should be there." Priestess looked at him vacantly. There was no guessing at the expression hidden behind his helm. "In time, that nest will grow, and then things will be worse. I have to nip it in the bud."

"So…so you're just going to abandon them?!"

"I don't know what you think I do," he replied with a steady shake of his head, "but this nest has to be taken care of. As I said, you can go to the forest if you want."

"B-but then you'll face the mountain nest alone, won't you?!"

"I've done it before."

"Ahhhh!" Priestess said, biting down hard on her lip.

Even from where she stood, Cow Girl could see Priestess shaking. But her face did not suggest fear.

"You're impossible!"

"You coming?"

"Of course I'm coming!"

"You heard her."

"Oh, thank you both so much!" Guild Girl said, bowing her head to them in gratitude. "No other experienced adventurers ever take on goblin quests…"

"Experienced, my foot," Priestess muttered sullenly, glancing down at her Porcelain tag. She looked like a pouting child.

"Ha-ha-ha… Well, you know… So, both of you are going?"

"Yes," Priestess said with a grudging nod. "Over my objections!"

He was always prepared, so with the administrative work done, they were set to depart immediately.

They were going to pass by Cow Girl on their way to the door. There was no other way out of the building. What should—or *shouldn't*—she say? Confounded, several times she opened her mouth as if to say something.

But in the end, she said nothing.

"I'm on my way." He was the one who, as always, stopped directly in front of her.

"What? Oh… Yeah." She gave a sure nod. There was a long pause before she managed to squeeze out two more words: "Be careful."

"You, too, on the way home."

Priestess nodded as she went past, and Cow Girl answered with an ambiguous smile.

He never looked back.

§

Cow Girl went back to the farm on her own, pulling the empty cart, and tended to the animals without a word.

As the sun climbed slowly but surely into the sky, she lunched on a sandwich in the pasture. And when the sun had slipped back toward the horizon, she ate dinner at the table with her uncle. She couldn't quite taste the food.

After dinner, she went outside. A cool wind born from the night brushed against her cheeks. When she looked up, she could see the whole vast sky with its many stars and two moons.

She didn't know much about adventurers or goblins. She hadn't been in her village when goblins attacked it ten years earlier.

She had been at her uncle's farm, helping with the birth of a calf. At her tender age, she didn't realize it was just an excuse to let her play.

It was sheer luck she had avoided the catastrophe. Just luck.

She didn't know what happened to her parents. She remembered burying two empty coffins. She remembered the priest saying something, but all she knew then was that her mother and father were gone.

She remembered being lonely at first, but she no longer felt it.

And there was always the *if.* If she hadn't fought with him that day. If she had asked him to come with her…

Maybe things would have been different. Maybe.

"Stay up too late, and you'll have a hard time tomorrow morning," a rough voice said over the sound of footsteps in the underbrush.

She turned and saw her uncle, with the same concerned expression he'd worn that morning. "I know. I'll go to bed in a little while," she promised, but her uncle shook his head with a frown.

"He has to take care of himself, but so do you. I let him stay here because he pays me, but it would be better if you kept away from him."

She was silent.

"I know you're old friends, but sometimes the past is just the past," he said. "He's not the same. He's out of control."

You should know that.

Cow Girl just smiled at his admonishment. "Maybe. But still…" She looked up at the stars. At the two moons and the road that stretched beneath them. There was still no sign of him.

"I'm going to wait a little longer."

He didn't come back that night.

It was noon the next day when he returned. Then he slept until dawn.

The day after that, showing no hint of fatigue, he joined Priestess in venturing to the southern woods. Cow Girl heard later that the rookies never returned from the forest.

That night, she had that familiar dream again.

She never had apologized.

CHAPTER 3

Guild Girl's Reflections

"Help us! You gotta help us! Them gubbins done come down to our village!"

"Filing a quest? Please fill out this form, sir."

The farmer clutched the paper so tightly it crumpled, and Guild Girl pulled out a fresh sheet. This was nothing unusual at the Adventurers Guild. She dealt with half a dozen people like this before breakfast.

Adventurers were busy during the day, so they mostly visited the Guild Hall in the morning or evening. Those filing quests, however, were not so predictable.

The battles among the gods had gone on so long that monsters were a familiar part of the world now. When a village was attacked, a nest of terrible creatures would inevitably be found in some nearby ruins or the like. The man before her that afternoon was just one more in a parade of people who showed up at their wits' end.

"If this goes on, gods know what's gonna happen to the poor cows! And our damn fields? The gubbins'll light 'em up…"

The farmer's hand quaked as he wrote. Each time he made a mistake, Guild Girl was ready with a new quest sheet.

Yes, each time—each time monsters appeared, each time they attacked a village, the adventurers would come. Be it dragons, demons, giant eyes with their unholy names, or sometimes even a crew of heartless outlaws.

All who stood among the age-old enemies of those who have words: the Unpraying.

Granted, this was a dubious term, since it included priests serving the Dark Gods. And most numerous among the Unpraying were— you guessed it—goblins.

"We ain't even got no young ladies for 'em to carry off!"

Guild Girl narrowed her eyes, trying to make sense of letters that crawled like worms across the page. They were hardly legible. This was the most talented scribe the village could muster?

Somehow it was always these tiny frontier farm towns the goblins went after. Were the goblins really targeting the villages on purpose? Was it just because there were so many villages—or so many goblins? As far as Guild Girl was concerned, such questions were above her pay grade.

"It looks like the paperwork is in order. Do you have the reward with you?"

"Sure enough. Say, is it true the gubbins take a girl sometimes and *get to know* her, then eat 'em?"

"There are cases where that has happened, sir."

The farmer was noticeably paler as he took out a sack. Guild Girl accepted it without a waver in her perfect smile. It was terribly heavy…

The sack was filled mostly with copper coins, a few silver ones shining among them. There wasn't a single gold coin in the bag.

Guild Girl took a set of scales from underneath the counter. The value of the coins would be measured against an established weight.

"All right, I've confirmed the amount," she said after a moment. "You're all set here."

She doubted whether the reward would even come to ten full gold pieces. Barely enough to hire a few Porcelain-rank adventurers at Guild rates. Take into account the processing fees the Guild charged for acting as an intermediary, and the farmers might actually be in the red.

But that mound of coins—some covered in dirt, some in rust, new and old pieces thrown in together—had meaning.

Someone who didn't understand that meaning could never become a Guild receptionist.

"Don't worry, sir. Some adventurers will be by within a few days to slay your goblins." No matter how she felt inside, her smile never faltered. The farmer nodded with relief.

He was probably picturing a monster hunter in resplendent armor, gallantly fighting off the goblins. Guild Girl knew better. She knew that was not who would show up. The adventurers who would find their way to that village would be Porcelain-ranked. Total beginners.

Most of them would be wounded in the battle. If things went poorly, they would die. There was even a chance that—worst-case scenario—the village would be destroyed.

So, while it might have been simply to make everyone feel better, all rewards were paid at the *end* of the quest.

There was no end to goblins. A proverb held that "each time a person fails, a goblin is born." They had only their numbers going for them. They were the weakest of all the monsters that might attack a village. Even trolls were no comparison.

Goblins had only the wits, strength, and physical size of small children. Then again, that's another way of saying goblins were every bit as smart, strong, and quick-witted as children.

Goblin slaying paid a pittance. Experienced adventurers avoided it like the plague.

Absolute newcomers were the only ones they could send.

They might be wounded, they might die, but they would kill the goblins. Even if the first party to go in was wiped out, the second or the third would come through.

Yes, the goblins would be driven out. Then the state wouldn't have to get involved. The state had bigger things to worry about: demons, general chaos.

"Well, miss, I sure am hopin'. Sure am hopin' you can help us."

Bureaucratic procedures finished, the farmer left the Guild building, bowing his head repeatedly in thanks. Guild Girl watched him go with a smile, holding back a sigh.

"This is the third one today..."

Send three parties of fledgling adventurers to their deaths, or let three villages be destroyed? Just thinking about it made her stomach knot. It hung over her like a cloud.

Of course, Guild Girl tried to explain things to all the rookies. She told them about the danger, even recommended other quests they could take.

But no one ever wanted their "adventure" to be killing rats in the sewers.

The experienced adventurers, for their part, were quite happy hunting down the creatures that lived in the mountains, far from any human habitation.

Very few adventurers who took on a goblin-slaying mission returned unscathed.

Mostly it was starry-eyed adventurers just starting out who took those assignments. The rest had just a modicum of experience. The Guild was forever troubled by its inability to produce a solid core of goblin fighters. And there simply were no accomplished adventurers who would willingly take on the immensely dangerous goblins.

"Well," she said to herself, stretching out across the counter, "that's not *quite* true." The cool, polished countertop felt good against her flushed forehead and cheeks. She understood it was not befitting either her upbringing as the daughter of a decent household or her station as a desk clerk at the Guild, but even she had to relax once in a while. And there were no visitors to see her just then, anyway.

I wish he'd hurry up and get here…

And at just that moment, the bell jangled as the door of the Guild opened. Guild Girl bolted upright.

"My dear Guild Girl, I have defeated some brigands!"

A spear-wielding adventurer came bursting through the entryway. The twisting expression on his face hardly looked happy. Behind him, a witch entered with mincing steps, her hips swaying as she walked. She met Guild Girl's eyes.

Witch winked at her apologetically. Guild Girl put that perpetual smile back on her face.

"Oh my, that sounds very tiring. Could you make your report, please?"

"Well, let me tell you, it wasn't easy! They were encamped right on the main road!"

"Oh my, that sounds very tiring. Please tell us all about it in your written report."

"There had to be at least twenty, twenty-one bandits holed up in there, and I took on every one!"

"Oh my, that sounds very tiring. Maybe you should try a Stamina potion."

"…Yes, please."

"Here you go. Thank you for shopping with us!"

The items the Guild sold on behalf of the merchants who frequented the place were, understandably, not of exceptionally high quality. The Stamina potion, for example, was not a proper magic potion but a brew of a few different herbs.

But it worked. There was no harm in keeping one on hand or even in actually drinking it. And the profit the Guild made on such items could be put to all sorts of useful purposes.

I'm never putting my face on that spot again, though, Guild Girl vowed to herself as, with a placating smile, she watched Spearman lean on the counter right where she had been lying a moment before.

That was when the bell rang a second time.

"Oh!"

"Ugh…"

The figure that appeared in the doorway made Guild Girl's face light up and Spearman give an unconcealed cluck of his tongue.

His stride was bold and unconcerned, somehow threatening violence.

He wore stained leather armor and a steel helm. His gear was cheap—pathetic even.

No one in the Guild Hall had to look at the silver tag around his neck to know who this was.

Goblin Slayer.

"Welcome back! Are you all right? No major injuries?"

"None to speak of."

Her pasted-on smile opened into a laugh like a flower bursting into bloom. As Spearman stood by with a choked expression, Goblin Slayer nodded and said:

"It was a small nest, but there was a hob there. Troublesome."

"I would love to hear all about it. Please have a seat, rest… Oh! I'll put on some tea, too!" Guild Girl ran like an excited puppy into the back office, her braid bouncing.

Goblin Slayer sat easily in a nearby chair, and he happened to glance at Spearman. For the first time, he seemed to realize Spearman had fixed him with a cold glare, and with a soft "hmph," Goblin Slayer said, "I apologize if I interrupted something."

There was a long pause. Then Spearman replied, "No, you didn't. I'd already finished making my report."

"I see."

The spear-wielding adventurer kicked a chair with a venomous grunt. On the bench facing him, Witch, who had watched everything, was waiting with a smirk.

"Brigands, you say? ...If we hadn't taken that road, we wouldn't have made a copper today."

"Oh, well, excuse *me*! So what if I wanted to brag a little?"

"Even if you say that...," said Guild Girl, her red lips creasing.

"So nothing. I think I recall my spells helping a bit, too...?"

"...I know they did."

"Aww, the Frontier's Strongest can't get pouty..."

Spearman crossed his arms sulkily. Witch, watching him fondly, gave a pleasant laugh.

Guild Girl snorted as she listened and mentally stuck out her tongue at them.

She knew, of course, that keeping bandit gangs under control was perfectly worthy work. And she knew Spearman, a Silver-ranked adventurer, was renowned by the name "the Frontier's Strongest."

So she didn't take him lightly, and she certainly didn't mean to brush him off. She really didn't *mean* to. It was just that—well, there are adventurers whose strength was their only claim to fame, and then there were those who went out of their way to take on the work nobody else would do.

How can I not treat them a little differently?

It wasn't just personal preference. For sure. Probably.

§

She set down the pretty clay mug with a *tap*. Steam rose from the light brown tea within.

When he drank it, Goblin Slayer appeared to be simply pouring the liquid into his helmet. He paid no heed to the fragrance or the flavor. Or the fact that the leaves were from her personal stock, which she'd gotten from the Capital and mixed with a bit of Stamina potion to create a unique brew…

"Um, anyway, welcome back!" Guild Girl said as sweetly as she was able. This was how he always was, so she tried not to be bothered by it. "I know you've been partied up with someone lately. Your first solo in such a long time must have been difficult."

"I always worked alone before. I can manage." He set the cup down with a nod. She was pleased at least to see there wasn't a drop left.

If nothing else, he's never said no to my tea.

"I see," she commented eagerly.

Well…it wasn't that there was nothing to complain about.

She was genuinely happy that he was mentoring that Priestess, whom Guild Girl had given up as hopeless. And she felt better just knowing that he had a companion in arms now.

But just him and a girl, all alone in some dungeon…? I don't know…

The one thing that gave her hope was knowing that he had always been more about work than women, and his friend was a devout cleric.

Assuming I haven't misjudged them.

Well, it was a little late to worry now, anyway. How long had he been living out on that farm?

In fact, Priestess had been off at the Temple for three days, claiming something about religious duties. Supposedly, she would be back to rejoin Goblin Slayer today or the following day…

Guild Girl smiled to herself. It was just like him to keep taking on quests by himself in the meantime.

"Something wrong?"

"Oh, no. Just…don't get yourself in trouble, all right?"

"If by getting myself in trouble I could kill some goblins, I would do it and not count it as a loss."

He was calm and, as ever, utterly focused on the slaying of goblins.

As she filled out some records, Guild Girl stole a glance at his helmet under the guise of looking at her paperwork. Of course, she couldn't see his expression. And yet…

How long had it been since she'd met him? Five years almost? She had just finished her training in the Capital and been officially assigned to this building.

He had shown up at the Guild suddenly, a beginner himself then. She was fairly sure that, at the time, she hadn't thought anything of it.

But whenever she couldn't move all the goblin-slaying quests, there he would be.

He always came back from those quests. And he always finished the job. Every single time.

He never showed off his strength or bragged about his accomplishments. He simply did what had to be done, again and again, until he eventually reached Silver rank.

He didn't take unnecessary risks; he was always kind, if quiet. It was worth the long, anxious waits for his return.

He hasn't changed his equipment since we met. But that's just another way of saying he's familiar.

Guild Girl realized the fond memories had caused her mouth to curl up in a smile, but she didn't try to hide it.

"Oh, you really are always such a big help."

"Am I?"

"Oh yes!"

There was a pause. "I see."

Guild Girl licked her thumb and paged through her papers, looking, as usual, for any goblin-related quests.

Yesterday he had killed goblins. Today he had killed goblins. There were plenty of beginner parties doing good work, too. And yet the goblin-slaying quests never ended. They got at least one every day. Maybe as adventurers multiplied, so did the goblin nests. Or maybe more goblin nests meant more adventurers.

"Why are goblins always attacking our villages?" Guild Girl asked idly. *It would be easier if it were the lizardmen, you know? Then, at least the only difference would be culture.* "Maybe goblins just enjoy attacking people." She thought she was just making conversation. Goblins were something they had in common. In fact, she was half joking.

"The reason?" he said. *It's simple.* After a pause, he continued, "Imagine that one day, your home is suddenly attacked by monsters."

Guild Girl straightened up and put her hands on her knees. She focused on her ears. She was ready to listen. After all, it wasn't often that he took it upon himself to talk.

*   *   *

"Imagine that one day your home is suddenly attacked by monsters.

"They swagger into your village like it belongs to them. They kill your friends, they kill your family, they loot your home.

"Imagine that they assault your sister. They torture her, they rape her, they kill her. They desecrate the bodies of your family, do whatever they want, cackling all the while.

"And you see it all from where you're hidden, trying not to breathe.

"How could you ever let that go?

"So you get a weapon, you train yourself, you learn, you grow. Everything you do is to help you take revenge.

"You search them out, hunt them down, you fight, you attack, and you kill them and kill them and kill them and kill them.

"Sometimes things go well, and sometimes they don't. But each time you ask—how will I kill them next time? What's the best way to kill them? Day after day, month after month, that is all you think about.

"When you get a chance, of course you test every idea you have.

"And when you've been doing all that long enough…

"…You start to enjoy it."

Guild Girl swallowed heavily.

"Um, is that…? Are you…?"

Was he still talking about goblins? She wasn't sure.

Maybe—the thought flitted at the edge of her mind—he was talking about himself.

But before she could voice this speculation, he continued, "Some fools think they're being magnanimous by saying we should spare the young ones." *Don't they realize the goblins steal livestock to keep those children fed?*

Shaking slightly, Guild Girl nodded. She understood what he was saying very well.

Porcelain rankers and young people wanting to be adventurers came all the time, brimming with confidence. *"I fought some goblins when they came to my village one time. They're small-fry. I'll be fine."*

The ones these village tough guys "fought" were no more than a few goblins, smoked out easily and set fleeing. Do that once or twice, and it left people thinking they ought to become adventurers.

The goblins that survived these encounters, on the other hand, would learn and grow. They were known as Wanderers. Many of them eventually settled in new nests, often as chieftains or guards.

After that, fights with them were determined less by strength than by luck.

"That's how things usually go, anyway," he said shortly. "In other words, I am to goblins what goblins are to us."

Guild Girl caught her breath, lost for words. What could she do with this torrent of emotion? No, first…first, there was him.

Good grief. She let her breath out. "Well, excuse me, but…"

"Yes?"

Before pity, before sadness, before sympathy: "We're the ones who give you your quests. So by your logic, what does that make us?"

"Erm."

Why do I feel so angry?

She pasted her usual smile on her face and tapped the counter with a finger.

"Are you comparing us to the Dark Gods? That's terrible. Am I really that scary?"

"…That's not what I meant."

"That's what it sounded like."

As she smacked the counter again, he gave an intimidated groan.

"How can the Guild keep up its reputation with talk like that going around?"

Another groan.

"I'd like to avoid that. Maybe it would be better if I didn't offer you quests in the future."

A long pause. "That would be a problem for me."

"Wouldn't it, though?"

Somehow his frank use of the word *problem* seemed very boyish.

Her fixed smile felt like it was about to shatter.

"Somebody has to do these quests, and you're doing them. You should be proud of that."

She wagged her finger as if to say, *If you aren't, it'll reflect on the Guild… and me.*

Noboru Kannatuki

It was true, after all. She was responsible for him as an adventurer. And what was more…

"You're a Silver-ranked adventurer."

This time, it was Goblin Slayer's turn to fall silent.

True, she couldn't see his expression behind his helm. But after five years, it didn't mean she couldn't guess how he was feeling.

Finally, he said, "And…where are the goblins today? How big are the nests?"

"All right, all right."

I guess I'll let him off…this time. As she giggled to herself, Guild Girl's fingers flew through the pile of quest papers. She pulled out three sheets, then picked one. It had been there for a few days—a goblin-slaying quest, of course.

"This one's up in the northern mountains. Near the village there's a—well, a castle, sort of. A mountain fortress."

"They've made their nest there?"

"Yes. We already have victims, too. The filer's sister was kidnapped, and…" She sighed as she flipped the paper over, though she knew it was bad form. "Some well-meaning adventurers who passed by went to rescue her, but they haven't returned."

"…It's too late," Goblin Slayer said calmly, coldly. "Considering how long the trip will take, they'll be lost before I get there."

Nonetheless, he stood. As ever, there was no sign of hesitation.

"We can't leave it. If we destroy the nest now, maybe there will be no more victims."

"…Right."

Right, that was it. That was why he was the most valuable person on the frontier.

There were those who could battle a powerful monster.

But how many could keep going back to the fight?

Many had been saved because of him. He was doing a real service to the world.

At the very least, he saved me.

So she would do what she had to. What she could.

"All right. Good luck, my Goblin Slayer!"

She would help him walk with his head held high.

CHAPTER 4

THE MOUNTAIN FORTRESS BURNS

After a feast that had lasted three days and three nights, the goblins were most satisfied.

The remains of their prey littered the floor of what had once been an opulent hall, now defiled with excrement and stench and corpses.

Before, they had made only one scrawny catch, but now they had four fresh prey. Four women, no less. Humans, of course, but also an elf and a rhea. The goblins were naturally elated about this, and their celebration was altogether without restraint—as if goblins ever showed restraint.

The girls were wildly outnumbered by the goblins, encircled, then completely surrounded by them... What happened next hardly bears repeating.

But these were not run-of-the-mill country girls.

The exposed bodies, clothes brutally torn away, were each different, but all showed the effects of long training. Their skin was sunbaked, with scars that spoke of old wounds, and each time they were played with, hardened muscles were visible through a layer of supple fat.

And in the corner of the room, thrust aside like so much garbage, was a pile of stolen armor and helmets, swords, and shields.

These women were adventurers of the eighth rank, Steel—or rather, had been.

Now, not one of them was breathing.

How did this happen?

That was the last thought to go through the mind of the noble daughter who had been the party's leader.

Had they been so wrong to take on this adventure, gripped by righteous indignation upon hearing about a village girl's kidnapping and wanting to set her free?

It wasn't precisely pride that had led to their destruction. They had snuck in at noon, hoping to catch the goblins as they slept.

The mountain fortress had been built of ancient trees by the elves, and it was a place unknown to the adventurers, a maze through which they had no guide. So they never let down their guard.

They prepared as well as they could in the small village, knowing full well many goblins awaited them. They simply knew they had to rescue the girl.

These were not fresh-faced beginners; they had been on a number of adventures and had a good deal of training and skill. In front, their armored leader held her weapon at the ready, and a rhea ranger watched the area like a hawk. Guarding their rear, an elven wizard was prepared with her spells, and a human monk prayed for miracles.

They had kept in formation, stayed alert, and checked every inch of ground. They had made no mistakes.

The cold, hard truth was they'd simply had bad luck.

First, the fortress—as was common in such structures—was full of booby traps. The traps the elves had once set to fend off goblins now, ironically, served to keep the goblins safe.

The exhaustion of their Ranger from searching out the elaborate, sensitive, and deadly traps played a large role in what happened. They had reached the inner sanctum of the fortress, and at the very end, Ranger missed a warning device.

"Everyone, form up!"

As an alarm echoed wildly, the party jumped to their places at their leader's command. Wizard stood in the center, with their leader, Knight, and Ranger and Monk at three points around her. It was no substitute for a good, solid wall between them and the enemy, but it was a strong formation.

But the goblins that surrounded them were so, so many.

Call it, if you will, the tyranny of the majority.

Ranger's archery skill was a divine gift, but even she couldn't hold out when there were more enemies than she had arrows.

Wizard used four of her arts, five—a great number—but eventually, her strength gave out.

Monk kept up her prayers for miracles and protection until she could pray no more, and she had nothing left.

Their leader fought on, her blade covered in blood, but as she tired, the goblins overpowered her, and then the hunt was over.

All those bodies—yet the fight could not have lasted a full hour.

And there among the heaps of arrow-pierced, sword-maimed, spell-burned corpses, a celebration began.

"Hr...hrrr..." The elf's voice was strained with fear.

"St-stay back... Stay back...!" The rhea's face was hopeless. Monk prayed soundlessly, and their leader was biting her lip hard enough to draw blood.

The goblins licked their lips as they stared down at their prey, who were huddling together and hugging themselves.

The party's third and final piece of bad luck was that their enemies were goblins.

Normally, goblin captives are either eaten or forced to become breeding vessels, and some are occasionally left alone, saved for a rainy day.

But this time was different.

These adventurers had killed many of their brothers, and no one was in the mood to give them an easy end.

Goblins lived by the law of survival, willing to sacrifice as many of their number as it took to win. So they did not grieve the deaths of their comrades. But anger and hatred at those deaths ran deep.

"GARUUURU."

"GAUA."

The goblins were delighted to find wine among the provisions they had taken from the women. Their drunken, small, mean minds invented one awful game after another to play with their prisoners. And the village was just down the mountain—an easy place to get more toys if they ran through what they had here.

The poor captured village girl had hardly served ten goblins before she could bear no more. They had used her up long ago.

There was no hope.

Knight, her clothes torn, a goblin holding her down, gave a howling scream.

"You bastards! You want to humiliate someone? Start with me!"

She was the daughter of a noble household. She had become a knight-errant in the service of the Supreme God, responsible for administering law and justice. She had contemplated every evil fate that might befall her and was ready for them.

But she was not prepared to sacrifice her friends.

First, Ranger was used for target practice before her eyes. The leader begged the goblins for her companion's life. Because Monk had attempted to bite off her own tongue when the goblins torturously killed her, they shoved her comrade's entrails into her mouth. When Wizard was burned alive, Knight's heart broke into a thousand pieces, and her soul failed her.

It was only after three days and three nights that the goblins at last granted the leader's wish.

What happened to her during those three days until her body, so mangled it barely looked human, was thrown into the river is not fit to be written.

The body of the adventurer that washed down to them, and the cackling laughter that echoed through the valley, left the villagers at the mountain's foot racked with fear.

But there are exceptions to every rule.

For example, one goblin on guard duty was holding a crude spear and patrolling the wall in the night air.

He, and he alone, was not laughing.

Obviously, it was not that he felt any kind of sympathy for the degraded women. He was simply upset that he had been left out of the celebration.

He had been on guard duty, watching the village, when the adventurers attacked, so he had not participated in the hunt. And (he was informed) he who does not hunt has no right to share the spoils.

He had no response to that argument, and so he had quietly withdrawn back to the wall.

The guard shivered at his post, freezing in the wind that blew down the mountain. Was it possible to draw a shorter straw?

They had spared him one burned finger. He would have at least liked a piece of the rhea. He chewed longingly on the finger, wishing for something more, and as he did, he began to breathe more and more heavily.

It didn't occur to him that if he had been in the fight with the adventurers instead of on guard duty, he might have died. Every goblin believes every other goblin will be out in front, while he himself fights from a comfortable spot in the back.

Still, the deaths of their brothers make them angry, and that makes them hard to handle…

"GUI…"

Never mind watching the village. Was a guard against encroaching enemies even necessary? This fortress had been built long ago by the elves (not that the goblins cared). When they left, it stood forgotten and deserted until the goblins moved in. All goblins want from a nest is that it be sturdy, safe, and offer good hunting. So they took over the fort, with all the traps, tricks, and walls its builders had left behind.

With all that, this fortress didn't need a guard. The goblin stuck on guard duty was deeply displeased.

So when he noticed them, he was actually thrilled.

"GRRRRR?"

Adventurers. Two of them.

One was a warrior in dirty leather armor and a steel helmet, making no attempt to hide himself as he strode calmly among the trees. A small shield was fastened to his arm. On his shoulder was a quiver, in his hand a bow, and at his hip a sword.

He looked like a weakling. Why should they worry about him? The guard goblin was focused on the person walking next to the warrior. It was a gorgeous girl in priestess vestments who stood awkwardly, clutching her staff and looking distinctly ill at ease.

The guard licked his lips. Neither of them was very meaty, but at least this prey he could get in on.

He made his ugliest face and, spittle dangling from his mouth, went back inside to alert the others. This was as per orders—but he should never have taken his eyes off the adventurers.

The warrior fitted an arrow into his bow and drew the string as far as he could. A rag soaked in Medea's Oil was wrapped around the arrowhead. Priestess struck a flint onto it.

"GAAU!"

"GOURR!"

The goblins the guard had summoned shuffled out onto the walls and began clamoring and pointing at the adventurers. But it was too late.

"Quite a crowd," Goblin Slayer muttered into his helmet as he loosed the arrow.

The bolt lodged in the wooden walls, and flames licked up toward the goblins, who began screaming.

A second burning shaft came flying. In the blink of an eye, there was fire everywhere.

"GAUAUAAAA?!"

One creature attempting to escape lost his footing in his panic and slipped, sending himself and two of his companions falling from the wall to the ground far below. The guard was among them, but Goblin Slayer neither knew nor cared.

"Three."

He counted calmly and let loose another arrow.

Fire, of course, was the great enemy of the elves. Had the forest people still been in that fortress, it would never have been so easy to attack with a simple burning rag.

But the elves, who would have offered supplications to the spirits to quench any flames, were no longer there. Any ward they might have erected against conflagration was long since gone.

The fortress in front of the adventurers was large and solid, but it was still just wood.

"That's enough fire arrows. Get ready."

"Oh, r-right!"

As Goblin Slayer drew his bow once more, Priestess stood with her sounding staff at the ready, prepared to begin the soul-effacing prayer to the goddess.

Covering her, Goblin Slayer put a bolt between the eyes of a goblin trying to flee the gorge. The monster tumbled backward into the burning fortress he had been so desperate to escape.

"Fool. That's four."

The next instant, there was a dull *clang* as a rock bounced off his helmet.

"Oh no! Are you all right?!" Priestess exclaimed.

"Don't panic," he replied with a shake of his head, annoyed that she had broken her concentration by shouting.

He clicked his tongue, then spotted a goblin in the gorge holding a rope.

A sling could be a powerful weapon. It might be just a bit of rope that flung a stone, but the projectile could travel with deadly speed and force. And it was almost impossible to run out of ammunition—a feature Goblin Slayer liked very much.

But anyway, even if the goblins had gotten ahold of a sling...

"It might matter in a cave. But not at this distance."

Outside of melee combat in confined quarters, the goblins' physical strength became irrelevant. They lacked the coordination for ranged attacks. The rock that had bounced off his helmet just now was probably a lucky hit.

Still, things might have been different if the two of them had been overconfident beginners. And Goblin Slayer was nothing if not thorough.

He launched an arrow in the slinger's direction, piercing him through the throat. Against the brilliant flames, the lack of night vision made no difference.

"Five... They'll be coming soon."

Just as he predicted, a crowd of goblins appeared in the entranceway, trying to flee the burning fortress. They carried their wine and their prey and their loot, and they shoved one another in their efforts to get out the door.

As they had run for their lives through the fortress, which they had grown rather fond of living in, it seemed their terror had turned to rage. Their hideous faces glowed with the lust to kill Goblin Slayer and Priestess. A great many evil plans ran through their heads. When they got out of the building, should they kill the two adventurers? Rape them?

Every goblin had a weapon in hand, and all of them were bent on Priestess standing just outside the entrance... ·

"O Earth Mother, abounding in mercy, by the power of the land, grant safety to we who are weak."

And suddenly the goblins found themselves slamming their heads against an invisible wall and rolling back into the fortress. A wall of holy power blocking the entrance and preventing the goblins' escape. The Earth Mother, abounding in mercy, had shielded her devout follower with the miracle of Protection.

"GORRR?!"

"GARRR?!"

The goblins grew increasingly panicked as they realized they'd been trapped. They screeched and cried as they beat their clubs and their fists against the invisible barrier and found nothing could break it. Smoke and flames slowly obscured the goblins, until they vanished from sight.

"I'd heard you'd been given a new miracle," Goblin Slayer said, casually shooting an arrow into a goblin trying to escape the area. "Six. It made our job much easier."

"But...to use Protection like this...," Priestess said. Her voice was hoarse, and it wasn't from breathing the smoke that rose from the once-living goblins.

She had been at the Temple the past several days in order to learn new miracles. Protection was one of two she had been given.

Depending on their strength and status, clerics who had gone out into the world might receive new miracles as well as oracles. It appeared her faith was stronger than even she herself had realized. It pained her each time the Mother Superior praised the fruits of her adventuring...

...But if it meant gaining a new miracle, she would endure the training in the belief that it would help her support Goblin Slayer.

And this was what had come of it.

Why did the Earth Mother allow me this miracle...?

She let out a long, miserable sigh.

"There might be a back door or an escape tunnel. Stay alert."

"How do you think of these things?"

"Imagination is a weapon, too." With those words, Goblin Slayer readied another arrow. "Those without it are the first to die."

"...You mean, like the people who came here earlier?"

"That's right."

The mountain fortress burned.

With that, the village below was saved from the threat of goblins. The souls of those departed adventurers could each go into the arms of whatever god they had believed in.

The bodies of the goblins burned. The bodies of the adventurers burned. And the body of the kidnapped girl burned as the smoke drifted into the sky.

"We'll have to control the blaze. When it's burned out, we'll need to look for any survivors and deal with them," Goblin Slayer said, looking up at the smoke, without a trace of emotion in his voice. There was a pause. "...Acting my rank can be...difficult."

Priestess watched him as though seeing something heartbreaking. There was no way she could know his expression under that helmet. Or there shouldn't have been.

Almost unconsciously, she joined her hands, knelt down, and prayed.

The heat and smoke covered the sky in dark clouds, and at length, a black rain began to fall. She prayed as the raindrops fell on her, as her vestments became streaked with ash.

The only thing she wanted was salvation.

Salvation for whom and from what she did not know.

§

"The Goblin King has lost his head to a critical hit most dire!"

The bard gave a warbling strum of his lute.

"Blue blazing, Goblin Slayer's steel shimmers in the fire."

The notes echoed around the evening street. People stopped to listen, drawn by the powerful yet melancholy tune.

"Thus, the king's repugnant plan comes to its fitting end, and lovely princess reaches out to her rescuer, her friend."

Young and old, men and women, rich and poor, people of every walk of life watched the bard. His peculiar epic would depend entirely on his own skill for its success.

"But he is Goblin Slayer! In no place does he abide, but sworn to wander, shall not have another by his side."

A young girl in the front row gave a warm, wistful sigh. The bard held back the smile that pulled at his lips and continued soberly:

"'Tis only air within her grasp the grateful maiden finds—the hero has departed, aye, with never a look behind."

Strum, strum, strum.

"Thank you! Tonight this is as far as I shall carry the story of the burning of the mountain fortress from the tale of the Goblin Slayer, hero of the frontier."

The audience that had gathered on that street in the Capital dispersed with a murmur. The bard gave an elegant bow of thanks as coins clattered into his cap.

A Silver-ranked adventurer who never suffered defeat as he drove out goblins all along the untamed frontier. To villagers beset by these monsters, he might as well have been of Platinum rank: a hero who appeared like the wind and left the same way. The epic the bard had fashioned about this figure from tidbits he'd chanced to overhear seemed to be well received. That was what counted.

"Sir...?"

Taken aback by the sudden, clear voice, the bard looked up in the midst of picking up some coins from the ground. The rest of the audience was gone, but one person stood there, face hidden by a cloak.

"That adventurer you were singing about... Does he really exist?"

"Of course he does. Absolutely." The bard puffed out his chest.

People *trusted* the deeds reported by the poets and minstrels. He could hardly admit he'd made up the song based on bits of accidental eavesdropping.

And anyway, this mysterious goblin killer had made him a good deal of money. The least he could do was see to the man's reputation.

"He's in a town two or three days' travel in the direction of the western border."

"Is that right?" the figure breathed, and with a nod, the hood of the cloak fell back.

Her supple body was clad in hunter's garb. A huge bow was slung across her back. She was slender and gorgeous.

The bard couldn't help staring—and not just because of her beauty.

He was struck by her long, leaf-shaped ears.

"*Orcbolg...*," she said, the sound melodious but strange. An elf adventurer.

GUILD GIRL

Yes, hello. Welcome to the Adventurers Guild! Filing a quest? Then, please…

Wh-what? An interview? Um…is this official? You're sure it's all right? Phew.

Ahem.

The Adventurers Guild; hee-hee, I know what you're thinking. It's weird to have an employment agency for a bunch of ruffians.

In reality, back at the very beginning, the Guild wasn't a guild—it was just a tavern where adventurers met. The King of Time established it to support those heroes—the people who would later be Platinum-ranked adventurers. But these days it's a real office! I passed an official examination and everything to become a receptionist, you know?

Professional women…hee-hee, my colleagues are all talented women, too, so I don't want to brag. But I was very lucky to get this job.

Adventurers work hard to gain the public's trust, because trust translates into better work. Our valued quest givers judge your abilities by your rank, and you're never shorted on payment.

And then, you know, there's— You've heard about this, right?

You get those traveling bullies who come in saying, "I've been *granted* a legendary weapon!" or "The gods themselves protect me!" They're really very difficult. They have no records, and we can't recommend our customers rely on people who go around doing whatever they want. It's not like we can just look at a sheet of convenient numbers and know how strong these vagabonds are.

That's why the Guild has established three bases on which to evaluate its members. Namely, how much good they've done in the world, the aggregate value of the rewards they've earned, and personality evaluations conducted via face-to-face interviews. Some refer to the collective result as "experience points."

This is what our rank structure looks like, with one being the highest and ten the lowest.

1. Platinum. This is extremely rare. Only a few people in history have attained this rank. Better not even think about it.
2. Gold
3. Silver
4. Copper. These ranks constitute our most talented members, as based on their abilities and the degree of trust they've earned. They're really something!
5. Ruby
6. Emerald
7. Sapphire. These are the middle ranks. Not many reach them these days.
8. Steel
9. Obsidian
10. Porcelain. These are our rookies. It's when they get comfortable that they're in the most danger.

You can see there are distinct lower, middle, and upper tiers. Call it a measuring stick.

What? Are there cases where a quest is ultimately never accepted? Well, I can't…say that there aren't…

It happens most often with goblin-slaying quests. There are so many of them, and the quest givers are often from farming villages, so… Well, they're not popular. They can be difficult, and the rewards are small. There are just so many goblins, you know?

I suppose you could say they're good beginner quests, but... Well...
Oh, excuse me, someone's just come in. Could we pick this up later?
Ahem!
Yes, hello! How can I help you?
"Give me goblins."

CHAPTER 5

UNEXPECTED VISITORS

"*Orcbolg*," the elf said without preamble. Her voice rang out clear, as if she were intoning a spell.

It was before noon, when the adventurers who had woken up late came to see what quests were still available. It was considerably calmer than first thing in the morning, but the Guild Hall was still filled with hubbub, and every eye was fixed on the elf.

"Oh, man… Get a load of her!" A greenhorn warrior boy whistled appreciatively.

"Hey!" his party member, an apprentice cleric girl, snapped.

"Sorry," the boy said with a placating smile, but his eyes kept darting back to the elf.

It was hard to blame him. Elves were naturally possessed of an otherworldly beauty, but even among their number, this young woman was striking.

Age has scant meaning for elves, but by appearance, she might have been taken for seventeen or eighteen years old. She was slender and tall, clad in close-fitting hunter's garb, moving as gracefully as a deer.

The great bow slung across her back showed she was a ranger or perhaps an archer. The rank tag around her neck was made of silver.

"She's a high elf… They're the blood descendants of the faeries…"

"Their ears really are longer than other elves'…"

A druid and a rhea girl whispered with a half-elf light warrior while their other party member, a heavy warrior, looked on. A young scout listening nearby said knowingly, "Of course they do."

Guild Girl had dealt with high elves before and was not nervous about meeting this one, but she was baffled by the words that came out of the girl's mouth.

"I'm sorry, ma'am. Do you mean *oak*, like the tree?"

She was used to people approaching the counter and simply saying the name of a monster, but this was a word she had never heard before. Then again, there are fifty thousand kinds of monsters (no exaggeration!), so it was possible this was some variety she wasn't familiar with.

Or perhaps it was the elf's name? The elvish language had the rhythm of a spell or a song.

"No. *Orc. Orcbolg.*" As she repeated the words, High Elf Archer tilted her head as if to say, *Got it?* Under her voice she added, "Strange…

"I'd heard he was here."

"Um, I see. So you're looking for an adventurer, then?" Guild Girl had many talents, but even she didn't know the full names of all the adventurers by heart. She turned to get a thick directory from the shelf behind her, but then she heard:

"Idiot. This is why you long-ears need to come down off that pedestal you've put yourselves on."

The words came from a stout, wide dwarf standing next to the elf. The only thing visible over the counter was his shiny, hairless forehead. He stroked his long white beard thoughtfully.

His outfit was in an unusual eastern style, and at his waist, he carried what looked like a bunch of junk. Guild Girl could tell he was a spell caster—a dwarf shaman. He, too, wore a silver tag around his neck.

"This place belongs to the tall people," he said. "More fool you if you think your long-ears words are going to profit you anything."

"My, how helpful you are. Then what, in your wisdom, *should* I call him?" the high elf said with a snort and a rather un-elven expression.

In response, Dwarf Shaman twisted his mustache proudly and said, "'Beard-cutter,' of course!"

"Um, I'm sorry, sir, but there's no one by that name here, either," Guild Girl said apologetically.

"What, no one?!" the dwarf said.

"No, sir. I'm very sorry."

The high elf shook her head in an exaggerated gesture of disgust, accompanied by a broad shrug and a sigh.

"So much for the wisdom of dwarves. Stubborn as the rocks they work, and always convinced they're right."

"Come down here and say that!" Dwarf Shaman exclaimed. He might have started a fight then and there if the elf hadn't been twice his height. He could barely have reached her if he'd jumped a foot off the ground. The elf grew increasingly smug.

The dwarf ground his teeth. Then suddenly, he seemed to think of something, and an unexpected smile came over his face.

"…Heh. You elves… Hearts as hard as anvils and just as flat. *That* explains it."

"What?!" This time it was the elf who turned bright red. She glared at the dwarf and unconsciously covered her chest.

"Th-that has nothing to do with anything! F-funny to hear that from you, when all dwarf daughters are barrel-shaped!"

"We call them *plump*, long-ears, and it's better than being an anvil!"

Their voices got louder and louder.

The enmity between elves and dwarves was as old as the gods. No one knew, however, exactly how it had started—even the ageless elves were not quite sure. Perhaps it was simply that most ancient antipathy: The elves revered trees and loathed fire, while the dwarves felled trees to build fires.

Whatever the source of this hatred, these two were not going to be the ones to overcome it, as they stood arguing in front of Guild Girl, who held an increasingly desperate smile on her face.

"Um, let's—let's all get along, okay…?"

"Excuse me, the two of you, but if you must quarrel, please do so elsewhere and spare the rest of us." A long shadow fell over them, interrupting the argument.

A lizardman towered over them, body covered in scales, hissing slightly foul breath. Even Guild Girl nearly let out a "yikes…" at the sight of him.

She had never seen the traditional garb he wore. Around his neck was a silver tag, as well as a curious amulet.

Lizard Priest joined his hands in an unusual gesture and bowed his head to Guild Girl. "Humble apologies. It seems my companions are causing trouble for you."

"Oh, n-not at all! All our adventurers are such passionate people. I-I'm used to this sort of thing!"

Even so, the group before her was an unusual sight. It wasn't just that they were different races.

High elves were rare, but it wasn't unheard of for young forest people to become adventurers to sate their curiosity about the world. Dwarves were much like humans in their love of treasure and derring-do, and so they often became adventurers. And while the lizardmen were sometimes seen as more akin to monsters, some of their tribes were friendly, and once in a great while, a lizardman might become an adventurer.

But all three at once—and all of them Silver-ranked. For three adventurers of such different backgrounds to form a party together was something Guild Girl had never seen before.

"Um..." Guild Girl looked from the elf and dwarf, whose argument had not yet abated, to the lizardman. Outwardly, he looked like he might bare his fangs and leap at her at any moment...

"So...who *are* you looking for, sir?" Even so, he seemed like the easiest of the three to talk to.

"Hmm. Lamentably, I myself lack facility for the tongues of men..."

Guild Girl nodded along.

"Orcbolg and Beard-cutter are what you would call nicknames. In your tongue, you might say..." He nodded gravely and, as she had somehow expected, said, "...Goblin Slayer."

"Oh!" Her face glowed, and she clapped her hands before she knew what she was doing. She suppressed the desire to give a shout of excitement.

Other adventurers had come here just to find him. His reputation was spreading.

I can't let this opportunity get away, for his sake!

"I know him, sir! Very well!"

"Ah, do you now?!" The lizardman's eyes widened and his tongue flitted out of his mouth, in what seemed to be the lizardman equivalent of a smile. Guild Girl didn't even flinch at the rather ferocious expression.

"Oh, would you like some tea perhaps?"

"I could not bother you so." He called to his companions, "The two of you, it seems the one we seek is indeed here."

"You see? I told you."

"Ahh, but you couldn't tell them, could you, lass?"

"Look who's talking."

"What's that?!"

Lizard Priest let out a hiss. The elf and dwarf glared silently at each other.

"Now then, milady Guild Girl. Where is milord Goblin Slayer?"

"Um… He went off to hunt some goblins about three days ago."

"Oh-ho. I see. But of course."

"I expect he'll be back soon, sir." Guild Girl looked hopefully at the door of the Guild Hall. She was worried about him, of course, but confident he would return.

He would never be defeated by mere goblins, after all.

"There!" Guild Girl called out as the bell over the door jangled, and two adventurers entered.

The lizardman, elf, and dwarf all turned toward the door…and were lost for words.

A beautiful girl in holy vestments stood there, holding a sounding staff in her hands. A priestess. Excellent.

The problem was the man who strode boldly before her. He wore dirty leather armor and a steel helm and carried a sword that seemed too long to wield, along with a small round shield. He looked pathetic. Any rookie on his first quest would have been better prepared.

He walked to the counter without a pause. Priestess had to rush to stay with him, but as his pace slowed, she was finally able to come to his side.

"Welcome back, my dear Goblin Slayer! Both of you look like you're in good shape." Guild Girl gave them a wide wave, her braid bouncing in time.

"We finished the job safely."

"Yes, somehow."

Priestess's addendum betrayed a hint of fatigue against Goblin Slayer's calm report. She was smiling bravely, but… Guild Girl nodded. She could understand. Goblin Slayer took quests day after day, night after night, with almost no rest. Keeping up with him must be trying.

"All right. Give me the details later. It doesn't have to be right away."

"Oh?"

"Yes. There are some visitors here to see you, Mr. Goblin Slayer."

He turned toward the party standing next to him as though noticing them for the first time: a high elf archer, a dwarf spell caster, and a lizard priest.

Priestess let out a little squeak of shock and then quickly shut her mouth.

"Are you goblins?"

"Hardly!" High Elf Archer gave him a suspicious look as if she couldn't believe what she was hearing, but he simply replied, "I see."

"So, are you Orcbolg? You don't look it…"

"Because I'm not. I have never been called by that name."

The elf got a pinched look on her face, while the dwarf, stroking his beard, bit back a laugh. Lizard Priest, though looking rather bothered, seemed accustomed to this. He joined his hands in an odd gesture, then bowed his head gently to Goblin Slayer.

"We humble visitors have business with milord Goblin Slayer. Could we beg a few morsels of your time?"

"As you wish."

"If you'd like to have a meeting, we have rooms upstairs…" The lizardman made a gesture of gratitude toward Guild Girl for her suggestion.

"Let us go, then."

Priestess had stood silently throughout the entire exchange but now said, with a slightly panicked look at Goblin Slayer as he made to leave, "U-um, sh-should I…? Should I j-join you?"

He looked up and down her slim body, then shook his head.

"You rest."

He didn't seem to expect an argument. Priestess gave a little nod.

And without a second look, Goblin Slayer went calmly up the stairs.

"Don't worry. You'll get him back in one piece." High Elf Archer gave Priestess a slight bow as she passed. The dwarf and the lizard-man followed after her.

Priestess stood there, alone.

§

"Sigh…"

All alone. She sat by the wall in the corner in the chair that seemed to be saved for him. Her hands wrapped around a cup of tea Guild Girl had brought her.

He probably just wanted what was best for her. She raised the cup to her lips.

"Ahh…" She sighed as a warmth spread through her body. Priestess had come to recognize this feeling as the effect of a Stamina potion.

It was kind of Guild Girl to add this to the tea. It felt wonderful to Priestess's tired body.

Am I holding him back?

He was of Silver rank, she merely Porcelain. Even despite this difference, she didn't think she was a burden to him, but still…

Priestess rubbed her eyes. Her eyelids were heavy.

She could hear the babble of adventurers throughout the Guild Hall. It was crowded as it was every day. Something tugged at the edge of her hearing, words she couldn't quite make out. She yawned.

"Hey! Hey there!"

"Whaa—?" When she heard the voice a second time, Priestess jolted awake, hurriedly straightening up.

Standing in front of her was a young man who looked somehow nervous—also Porcelain-ranked.

He was a greenhorn warrior she'd seen around before. Standing next to him was a girl, an apprentice cleric. From her neck hung the scales and sword, the symbols of the Supreme God, who oversaw law and justice.

"You… I mean, you're the girl who works with him, right?"

"With…who?"

"You know, that guy. He's always wearing that helmet?" the cleric said in a high-pitched voice.

"Oh," Priestess said, her puzzlement evaporating. "You mean Mr. Goblin Slayer?"

"Yeah, that's him! Hey…" Warrior suddenly dropped his voice and looked around fearfully. "You're Porcelain-ranked, too. How about you come with us?"

Priestess caught her breath, silent. A torrent of emotions raged within her, threatening to split her heart in two.

She clenched her fists and pushed back the onslaught. It was only a second before she slowly shook her head.

"No. Thank you, but no."

"But he's a weirdo! What kind of Silver rank hunts nothing but goblins?" Warrior asked frowning. *Any normal Silver rank would go after bigger stuff.*

"Yeah," Cleric said, peering around the room with concern herself. "And dragging around a rookie, too. You know some people think you're his prisoner?" *Are you all right?*

"I even heard the reason he goes off hunting goblins by himself is something…*weird*. Know what I mean?"

"Now, that's not—!" Priestess's voice rose reflexively.

"Now, now. *No* bullying." Their collective emotions were soothed by a gentle, sweet voice that suddenly broke in. When had she gotten there? How long had she been there? Witch, with her sensuous body and a silver tag around her neck, was standing right next to them.

"B-but we weren't—"

"That, will be enough. Go, over there, okay?"

Warrior looked like he was ready to argue some more, but Cleric took him by the sleeve and led him away.

Witch gave Priestess a friendly look and said with a smile, "Let me, handle them, yes?"

That was all it took. Cleric and Warrior said, "Let's get out of here!" seemingly at the same time, and with an anxious look at Priestess, they left.

Priestess sat in her chair, teacup in her hands. Witch slid into the chair next to her, almost pouring herself into the seat.

"So, then. You *are*, the girl who tags along, with him, yes?"

"Oh yes, ma'am, I am allowed the honor of accompanying him."

Priestess nodded firmly, settling her hands along with the teacup on her knees.

"*Accompany*, eh?" Witch said meaningfully. Priestess gave her a puzzled look. Witch waved it away. "It must be, quite, difficult. He doesn't *notice* much, does he…?"

Priestess gave her the puzzled look again. "Um, I… He…"

"Then again, it seems, you're not much better."

Priestess made an apologetic gesture of embarrassment, and Witch looked at her fondly. She produced a long metal pipe and put some leaves into it with an elegant hand.

"May I? …*Inflammarae*." Without waiting for an answer, Witch tapped the pipe with her finger. A fragrant pink smoke soon drifted out of it.

"I know. A silly waste of a word of power, isn't it?" Witch gave a spontaneous laugh at the dumbfounded Priestess. "And you… How many miracles, can you use…?"

"Um, I had two until recently; now I have four. I can only pray about three times, though…"

"A Porcelain rank, with four miracles. My, you're quite accomplished."

"Oh, th-thank you…" Priestess bowed her head, making her small body appear even smaller. Witch's smile didn't waver.

"You know, he once, made a rather strange request, of me, too."

"What…?" Priestess suddenly glanced up at Witch's face.

Witch cocked her head alluringly. "I know, what you're thinking," she said teasingly.

"N-no, I'm not…!"

"He wanted a little help, with a scroll. So I know how, difficult it is, to…*accompany* him."

"No, I… He… Well, a little. He is Silver rank, after all." She gave a slight, tired frown. When her head nodded, she saw the teacup still in her hands. Looking at the bottom of the cup through the translucent brown liquid, the words seemed to drop from her lips like water:

"I-I can barely even keep up with him… And I-I'm nothing but trouble for him…"

"And he's so, good at what he does, isn't he?" Witch breathed deeply and blew out a smoke ring. It floated lazily over to Priestess and dissolved against her cheek. She coughed violently. Witch apologized with a laugh.

"That's what, comes with years, and years, hunting goblins, without rest." *He's leagues ahead of a Porcelain-ranked girl.* Witch spun her pipe thoughtfully. "Goblin slaying certainly, does more good in the world, than someone who hunts bigger prey...but isn't any good at it." Her pipe indicated the adventurers milling about inside the Guild Hall.

Somewhere in the hall, Spearman's ears burned. Witch narrowed her eyes and looked out into the crowd.

"That's not to say, a fixation, on goblins is...entirely, healthy."

Priestess was silent.

"In the Capital, for example, there's no end of demons. There are monsters, everywhere, in this world."

Well, obviously. If there weren't, adventurers would not have been so ubiquitous, no matter how many abandoned ruins there might be. But with threats of every type popping up in every place, the military alone couldn't keep things under control. Their role was supposed to be dealing with neighboring countries, or Dark Gods or necromancers. Goblins were clearly a threat. But they weren't the only one.

"If you want to...help someone else. You can do that, even with, those two children from earlier, for example."

"That is— I could, but..." Priestess was growing agitated again. She leaned forward in her chair, but she couldn't get any more words out. She trailed off with an incoherent mumble.

"Hee-hee. There are, so many, paths, yes? And no, certainties. It's difficult indeed..." She gave the huddling Priestess a pat on the head. "I'm sorry." Priestess found the sweet-smelling smoke oddly calming.

"At the least...if you're going to, *accompany* him, let it be, your own decision."

If you'll forgive my saying so.

With that, Witch stood up with the same slinking motion as when she'd sat down.

"Oh..."

"I'll, see you. I do believe you have, a date—pardon me, an adventure— with him." And with a slight wave of her hand, she walked away, hips swaying, and vanished into the crowd.

"My own decision…?"

Alone again, Priestess gently worked the teacup around in her hands. The warmth she'd felt moments before was gone.

§

As they entered the meeting room, the elf unslung her bow from her shoulder and asked, "So, are you really Silver rank?"

The chairs in the room were covered in bronze-colored cloth and surrounded a table that had been polished to a shine. The shelves were lined with monster skulls and fangs, the trophies of past adventurers.

"According to the Guild." Goblin Slayer's filthy armor and helmet hardly seemed to speak to his rank. He sat down heavily in a chair.

"Frankly, I can't quite believe it," the elf said. She sat across from him with barely so much as a footfall and shook her head. "I mean, look at you. I've seen bugs that looked more intimidating."

"Don't be stupid, long-ears!" The dwarf, happily seated cross-legged on the floor, gave a derisive laugh. Though humans tried to be considerate of other races, their chairs were too large for dwarves and rheas. "Before they're polished, jewels and precious metals all look like rocks. No dwarf would judge a thing by its appearance alone."

"Oh, really?"

"Yes, really! Leather armor prizes ease of movement. Mail would stop a dagger in the dark," Dwarf Shaman pontificated, appraising Goblin Slayer with a wide look. Though most of his duties were pastoral, when it came to weapons and equipment, even a dwarf child knew more than many a long-lived shopkeeper. "…His helmet, the same. Sword and shield are small, easy to use in a tight space."

Goblin Slayer said nothing.

The elf looked suspiciously at him.

"He could at least get nicer-looking equipment."

"Clean items reek of metal," Goblin Slayer said, a note of annoyance in his voice. *Goblins have an excellent sense of smell.*

"Gods. You forest dwellers are so in love with your bows, you wouldn't know a sword if it was stabbing you in the neck."

"Ergh…" The elf ground her teeth at the dwarf's barb. He was obnoxious, but not wrong. Hunting came as naturally as breathing to the elves. This archer, for her part, did know something about suppressing smells. But she was young among the high elves and had left her home forest only recently. The several years she had spent so far in the wider world were the blink of an eye for an elf. She still lacked much experience.

The dwarf stroked his beard with a self-satisfied look. "My life has been longer than your ears, girl. Why don't you learn something from your venerable elder?"

"Hmph." But then the elf narrowed her eyes like a cat playing with a mouse. "I'm two thousand years old," she said. "How old are you again?"

The dwarf said nothing for a long moment. Then, reluctantly: "One hundred and seven."

"Oh my, oh my." The elf snickered, and the dwarf stroked his beard dejectedly.

They seemed set to go on that way forever. Just as Goblin Slayer was beginning to think it time for him to go back downstairs, Lizard Priest gave an agitated wave of his hand.

"The two of you, that is enough talk of your antiquity. You shame those of us who do not measure our lives in centuries or millennia." He was standing against the wall. Lizardmen did not sit in human chairs, mainly, it seemed, because their tails got in the way.

"Now, what do you want with me? A quest?" Goblin Slayer was to the point as ever.

"Yes, that's it," the elf said. She looked grave. "The number of demons around the Capital has been growing, as I'm sure you know..."

"No, I don't."

"This can be traced back to the revival of the evil spirits. They want to use an army to destroy the world!"

"I see."

"...And we were hoping, with your help..."

"Find someone else," he said bluntly. "If it isn't goblins, then I don't care."

The elf stiffened. "Do you understand what I'm saying?" she asked through gritted teeth, an undercurrent of anger in her voice. Her distinctive, leaf-shaped ears trembled. "An *army of demons* is coming. We're talking about the fate of the world here!"

"Yes, I heard you."

"Then why—?"

"Before the world ends, the goblins will put an end to many more villages," Goblin Slayer told her in his even, almost mechanical voice. As if to say, *This is my everything, my truth.* "We cannot ignore the goblins because the world is in danger."

"How can you—?!" The elf kicked her chair, her pale face gone red. She leaned over the table to grab hold of Goblin Slayer. It was the dwarf who stopped her.

"Well now, hold on, long-ears, think about what you're doing."

"What do you mean, dwarf?"

"We all can't just barge in here and order him to do something. A Platinum might get away with that, but not us."

"Ye— Well, yes, but…"

"No buts, then. Settle down. Let's have us a nice, civil chat." He chided the elf with a wave of his small, rough hand.

"…Fine," she huffed grudgingly and settled back in her chair. Seeing this, and seeing that Goblin Slayer did not seem the least bit upset by the incident, the dwarf gave a satisfied laugh.

"He may be young, but he is 'Beard-cutter' indeed! He's as settled as stone!"

"Then," Lizard Priest said, "you will not object if I proceed to offer him this quest?"

"Fine by me," the dwarf said, running his hand through his beard. "Better this than a coward."

"Milord Goblin Slayer, please do not mistake our meaning. We have, in fact, come to ask you to help us slay the small devils."

"I see. So you are talking about goblins," Goblin Slayer said. "In that case, I accept."

There was silence.

"Where are they? How many?"

High Elf Archer looked slightly aghast; Lizard Priest's eyes widened. The dwarf laughed vigorously.

"Well now, what's the rush, boy? Don't you want to hear the rest of Scaly's story?"

"Of course," Goblin Slayer said with a firm nod. "Information is crucial. I need to know the size of the nest, whether there's a shaman. What about hobs?"

"I had expected you might ask first about remuneration," Lizard Priest said, his tongue flicking out and touching his nose. It might have been like covering his face to hide his embarrassment. "...To begin with, as my humble companion said earlier, there is an army of demons readying to invade."

Silence.

"One of the Demon Lords, heretofore sealed away, has awakened and now seeks to exterminate us..."

"Not interested," Goblin Slayer said. "The same thing happened ten years ago."

"Mm. I, too, thought it did not concern me." The lizardman rolled his eyes around with a grimace.

A variety of expressions played over the elf's face as he spoke, mostly communicating *I can't believe this guy.* She glowered at Goblin Slayer, but his face, and any expression, was hidden behind his helm.

"But thereupon the chieftains of our tribes, all the kings of men, and the leaders of the elves and the dwarves held a great conference."

"Rheas aren't much for combat, so we lack one—but otherwise, we are the representatives they've sent," the dwarf said, pounding his belly. "We are adventurers, after all. We'll do the world and our ranks some good as a part of the bargain!"

"It looks like we're headed for a huge battle." *Not that you care.* The elf seemed to have given up.

The dwarf continued, stroking his beard. "The problem, see, is those nasty little buggers have started growing more active in elf lands."

"Have any champions or lords emerged?" Goblin Slayer asked in a murmur.

The dwarf replied, "Perhaps."

The elf perked up her long ears at the unfamiliar words. "Champions? Lords? What are those?"

"Goblin heroes. Goblin kings. Think of them as Platinum-ranked goblins, in our terms." Goblin Slayer folded his arms with a long "hmmm." He seemed very serious. The elf thought he appeared to be calculating something. After a long pause, he said:

"Never mind. Not enough information yet. Go on."

"Upon our investigation, we discovered a single, exceptionally large nest. But…well, politics, you know."

"The military won't move against goblins. As ever." Picking up the lizardman's thought, Goblin Slayer seemed to ask and to affirm at the same time.

"The human kings see us as allies, but not equals," the elf said, her shoulders stiff. "If we tried to bring our soldiers into this, they would think we were plotting something."

"Hence, a party of adventurers… But we alone could hardly stand before the humans."

"So, Orcbolg… Out of the many, we have chosen you."

"Long-ears has a real way with words, doesn't she?" the dwarf said with a dry laugh. The elf glared at him, but the look passed quickly.

"Do you have a map?" Goblin Slayer asked calmly.

"Here." The lizardman took a scroll from his sleeve and handed it to Goblin Slayer. Goblin Slayer unrolled it with a rough hand. The map was drawn in dye on tree bark. The abstract yet precise style was typical of elvish cartography.

It depicted a barren field with an ancient-looking building. Goblin Slayer pointed to the structure.

"Ruins?"

"Probably."

"Number?"

"We only know the nest is very large."

"I'll leave immediately. Pay me what you like." Goblin Slayer nodded, rolled the map up with a casual motion, and stood forcefully. Stuffing the map away, he made a rapid check of his equipment and then began to stride toward the door.

The elf grew agitated. "W-wait a second!" Her ears flicked, and as before, she kicked her chair and reached out her hand. "You sound like you're going to go out there alone."

"I am."

The elf's frown said, *You've got to be kidding.*

The lizardman made an intrigued noise. "This is only my humble observation, but that esteemed acolyte of the Earth Mother is a party member of yours, is she not, milord Goblin Slayer?"

"You're going to take them on alone?" the elf said. "Are you insane?"

Goblin Slayer stopped and exhaled slowly. "Yes."

And without another word, he walked out of the meeting room.

Which question he had meant to answer, they could not tell.

There was no way they could know.

§

Inhale, exhale. He paused for only a second. Then Goblin Slayer walked briskly down the stairs and straight up to the front desk. The word he uttered was the same one that was always on his lips:

"Goblins."

"So they did come to offer you a quest!" Guild Girl looked up brightly from her work.

Spearman clucked his tongue nearby. He had just been trying to talk to Guild Girl.

"What kind of quest is it? I'll make a record."

"That lizardman will give you the details. I'm heading out. But I need money. Give me the reward from the last quest."

"Hmm... But you haven't made your report yet... Well, I suppose for you we can make an exception, Mr. Goblin Slayer." She added, "Just between you and me." She signed a piece of paper and took a leather pouch out of a safe. A reward that might not be enough to compensate even a Porcelain-ranked party could be a pretty fair sum if you took on the entire adventure yourself. Goblin Slayer could support himself on goblin-quest pay precisely because he worked alone.

He took the pile of dirty coins—painstakingly collected by the inhabitants of some impoverished village—and slid half into his purse.

"Give the rest to her."

"Sure. W-wait, are you alone? Isn't she—?"

"I'm letting her rest."

That was all he said to the mystified Guild Girl before walking away.

Spearman shot Goblin Slayer a dirty look as he walked by.

"What does he think he's on about, anyway?"

But Goblin Slayer didn't hear the sneering whisper. It didn't matter. He had a great deal to think about.

As he walked, he was mentally calculating his remaining supplies. He would have to buy rope, wedges, oil, antidotes, potions, and a number of other consumables. Once he got out of the Guild Hall, he would have to go somewhere to stock up on provisions as well. He needed his energy. Camping gear was no problem. As long as he was by himself, the most minimal comforts would suffice. Assuming the scroll was correct—

"Mr. Goblin Slayer!"

As he was about to walk out the door, he heard light footsteps hurrying after him. He snorted.

"Um, that—that was a quest, right?"

It was Priestess.

It was not very far from her chair to the door, but the run seemed to have tired her. She was breathing hard and her face was red.

"Yes," he said. "Goblin slaying."

"That's...what I thought." Priestess gave a resigned smile. She could barely keep up with his unpredictable coming and going. Nonetheless, she held up her sounding staff excitedly. "Then just let me—"

"No." Goblin Slayer cut her off coldly. "I'll go alone."

"What?!" Priestess raised her voice at Goblin Slayer's calm words.

Every eye still in the hall turned toward them at her near-scream. Some muttered, "Oh, it's Goblin Slayer," and looked away again.

But Priestess stared straight at him, flinging her words. He would *not* go alone. She didn't care if he always came back. He would *not*.

"At least—at least you could talk to me before you decide—"

Goblin Slayer cocked his head in an expression of complete bafflement. "Aren't I?"

Priestess blinked.

"I...I guess we're talking, yes…"

"I believe we are."

"Ahh…" Who could blame her for the sigh that escaped her at that moment?

"But it hardly means anything if I don't have any choice in the matter, anyway."

"It doesn't?"

He's really hopeless.

"I'm going with you." She declared it bravely, without hesitation.

From the other side of his visor, Goblin Slayer looked at her. His dirty, battered helmet was reflected in her stare.

"I can't leave you," she said.

Their eyes met. Both were silent for a long moment.

"…Do what you want." Finally, Goblin Slayer heaved a sigh. He sounded a bit annoyed.

But Priestess held her staff with both hands. Her smile was like a blossoming flower.

"Thank you, I will."

"Then go collect your reward first."

"Right! Just wait here a moment… Hey, what about our report?"

"We can do it later."

"All right!"

Goblin Slayer stood by the door and waited as Priestess ran off. From the landing, uncommon faces watched her. High Elf Archer, Dwarf Shaman, and Lizard Priest all looked at one another. Someone let out a tiny sigh.

"Even we can see what's going on here. That girl's got promise." The dwarf was the first to come down the stairs, stroking his beard.

"Far be it from me to propose a quest and refuse to offer myself in pursuing it." The lizardman came next with a stern nod, joining his hands toward the elf. He descended the stairs a step at a time, his tail swishing back and forth.

The archer was silent, lost for words.

Orcbolg, the goblin-slaying adventurer, was here before her eyes, yet he was nothing like she'd imagined. She couldn't comprehend his way of life. He was alien to her.

What, are you going to let a little shock stop you now?
The elf laughed. Hadn't she left the forest looking for exactly this?
She checked her bow and then secured it across her shoulder.
"Grief, don't you think you should respect your elders?"
So saying, she stepped lightly down the stairs.
You see, parties are often formed in just such unexpected ways.

Hmm? An interview...? Goblin slaying? What a strange thing to ask about.

Some goblins attack a village. The villagers come to us. *Please get rid of the nest. Help us! We beg you, O heroes!* So we get our weapons, go in there, kill a few goblins, and get our money. What's to talk about? Your basic hack and slash.

It's quick work. I won't deny we were lucky, too, but... Well. You get some experience in tracking and fighting, and the Guild gives you a surprising amount of credit for helping out. I mean, I understand. My hometown was attacked by goblins not long ago. And it's true, some adventurers came to help out.

It's just... How do I say this? There are three types of people who hunt goblins: People who beat them easily. People who take their lumps and learn from them. And people who underestimate the goblins and get wiped.

Which are we? We beat them easily! Well...anyway, we do now. We took our licks before. We brought a lantern in with us, but our scout fell and broke it. Then everything was pitch-dark. We found out later the goblins had planted a trip wire. A trap. Goblins set a trap!

The light and the noise gave away our position, and once things went dark, there were goblins everywhere.

The kid—our magic user—got a little worried and tried a spell.

"Don't do it," I says. "Save it for something big. You've only got one. Don't waste it on some shrimp monster." After that, all hell broke loose.

Goblins all around us. We're fighting as hard as we can, slice, slice, slice. Death. Screams. You don't know if you're hitting rocks or cutting flesh. You've been cut, too. You're just wearing cheap armor. When I found myself trying to swing a broadsword in a tunnel, that's when I thought I was going to die.

Hey, what are you smiling at, dammit? The greatest warriors started out risking their lives against goblins. You want to be a paladin, don't you laugh.

Sorry about that. That lady—that knight—is in my party. I'm the leader, though, all right?

Where was I? There was a big one leading them. My sword got caught on something. He had an ax, and he's swinging it everywhere. I thought for sure I was gonna die. Then *wham*, a Firebolt fries him.

Our knight had some miracles; we had money, got equipment and antidotes and everything. It practically cost more to get ready than we got for doing the quest…but it saved me. It saved all of us.

That's why I always say, as long as you're prepared, goblins ain't nothing.

But say you knew you could win ninety-nine times out of a hundred. Who's to say this isn't the hundredth time? There's no guarantees. You're just playing the odds.

If you're gonna die because of a bad roll, you might as well do it fighting a dragon.

And we're Silver-ranked now. Grunt work like goblins won't keep our party equipped.

Anyway, goblins are the weakest monsters, right? So why not let beginners handle 'em? Sure, not all of them make it, but…they've got better chances than against a dragon, right?

Still…it's only a chance.

CHAPTER 6

TRAVELING COMPANIONS

Three days passed in the blink of an eye.

Beneath the stars and the two moons, in a field that seemed to go on forever, five adventurers sat in a circle. A long, thin trail of smoke drifted into the air from their campfire. Far behind them, the forest where the elves lived rose up in the darkness.

"Come to think of it, why did all of you become adventurers?"

"For the fine dining, obviously! What about you, long-ears?"

"Of course you wanted food. Me...I wanted to learn about the outside world."

"As for myself, I seek to raise my status by rooting out heresy, that I may become a naga."

"Say what?"

"I seek to raise my status by rooting out heresy, that I may become a naga."

"Uh... Sure. I can understand that, I guess. I'm religious, too."

"I wanted to slay..."

"Yeah, somehow I think I've got you figured out, thanks."

"Don't interrupt the man, long-ears!" The dwarf gave a cluck as he wove blades of dry grass together.

The fire did not burn very high. The elves hated fire and set wards to keep what burns at bay. Even as far from the forest as they were, the effects were still noticeable.

Priestess and the lizardman had prepared this, the last dinner they would eat before they reached the nest.

"Mmm, that is delicious! What is this?" The well-marbled meat had been finished with spices as soon as it began to roast. The dwarf, delighted by the fragrant, crunchy result, took two or three skewers.

"I am pleased you find it satisfying." The lizardman replied to the dwarf's praises with a gratified smile, which for him meant baring his long teeth. "It is the dried flesh of a swamp creature. The spices include ingredients not found in this place, hence why your palate may find them remarkable."

"This is why no one likes dwarves. They're gluttons and carnivores to boot," the elf scoffed.

"Bah! How could a would-be rabbit like you appreciate the virtues of a meal like this? Hand me another!"

"Ick…"

The dwarf licked the fat from his fingers and took another large mouthful of meat as if to underscore his point. The elf groaned from watching him consume so vigorously something she couldn't even contemplate eating.

"Um, maybe you would like some soup? It's not much, with only a campfire to cook over, but…"

"Yes, please!"

Priestess made a soup of dried beans with a practiced hand. The elf hadn't had any of the meat, so the suggestion of something she could eat was enough to make her ears bounce for joy.

The brimming bowlful of soup Priestess passed her had a mild flavor that was undeniably delicious.

"Hmm. I've got to give you something for this…" The elf took small, thin wafers of bread wrapped in leaves from her pack and broke off a piece. The smell of it was faintly sweet, but it had no fruit or sugar in it.

"This…isn't dried bread, is it? And it's not a biscuit…"

"It's a preserved food the elves make. Actually, we almost never share it with anyone else. But today is an exception."

"This is delicious!" No sooner had she taken a bite than the striking taste brought words of appreciation from Priestess's lips.

A little surprise was hidden in the food. The crispy outside gave way to a soft, moist center.

"Oh? That's good." The elf affected disinterest, but the way she closed her eyes slightly made her look quite pleased.

"Hrm! Well, now that the elf is showing off, I can hardly let the dwarves go unrepresented, can I?" Thus Dwarf Shaman produced a large, tightly sealed clay jar. There was a sound of liquid sloshing within. When he pulled out the stopper and poured some into a cup, the pungent scent of alcohol drifted around the camp.

"Heh-heh. Say hello to our specialty, made deep in our cellars—fire wine!"

"Fire...wine?" The elf looked with interest into the cup the dwarf held out.

"Nothing less! Tell me this isn't your first tipple, long-ears."

"O-of course not, cave dweller!" So saying, she snatched the cup out of his hand.

She cast a doubtful look into the seemingly ordinary cup. "It's clear. Isn't wine made from grapes? I've had it before, you know. I'm not *that* young." She threw back her head and drank the entire cup.

There followed a fit of uncontrollable coughing, brought on by the drink's stinging dryness.

"A-are you all right? H-here, have some w-water!" Priestess hurriedly offered a canteen to the gasping elf, whose eyes were bulging.

"Ha-ha-ha-ha-ha! Maybe it's a bit too much for a delicate lass like yourself!"

"Please be temperate. A drunken ranger will avail us little."

"I know that, Scaly! I won't let her have too much."

The dwarf laughed merrily at the women while the lizardman hissed reprovingly.

"Ho there, Beard-cutter! Fancy a sip?"

Goblin Slayer said nothing but took the proffered cup and drank it with alacrity.

He had not spoken a word all through dinner, merely lifting food into his visor. Soon after, he became absorbed in his own work. He polished his sword, shield, and dagger; checked the sharpness of the blades; and returned them to their sheaths. He oiled his leather and mail armor.

"Hrm…" The elf made a dissatisfied noise at the sight of Goblin Slayer at his tasks. Her face was as red as a boiled tomato.

"…What?"

"…You don't even take that helmet off when you're eating. What's with you?"

"If I were to be struck in the head by a surprise attack, I might lose consciousness."

"…And y' jus ead, ead, eat. Why dun you cook sumtheng for us arready?"

The elf delivered this non sequitur with a heavy tongue, slurring her words. She pointed accusingly at the large rock next to Goblin Slayer.

He did not respond, even when the drunken elf glared at him and issued another "Hrrmm?"

"Ooh," the dwarf whispered. "Her eyes are glazing…"

Watching the scene, Priestess sucked in her cheeks slightly.

He's thinking. She still couldn't see his face, but she knew that much.

After a time, Goblin Slayer sought out his pack with a hint of exasperation. He rolled out a dry, hard round of cheese.

"Will this do?"

Oh-ho. The lizardman licked the tip of his nose with his tongue. He craned his neck toward the cheese as though he had never seen it before.

"What manner of thing is this?"

"It's cheese. It's made by churning the milk of a cow or a sheep."

"You've got to be joking, Scaly," the dwarf said. "Never seen cheese before?"

"I am most earnest. This is quite new to me."

"Do lizardmen not raise livestock?" Priestess asked. He nodded.

"In our society, animals are for hunting. Not for nurturing."

"Give it 'ere. I'll cut it." The elf swiped the cheese from Goblin Slayer and, almost faster than the eye could see, sliced it into five pieces with a knife she had sharpened on a rock.

"I bet a little grilling would do wonders here. Now, where's a good stick?"

At the dwarf's suggestion, Priestess said, "I have skewers if you like." She took several long metal rods from her bag.

"Ah, lass, you know how to pack for a trip! Unlike *some* people I know."

"If you've got someone in mind, come out and say it." Anger seemed to put the clarity back in the elf's voice.

"Why don't you ask your heart?" The dwarf chuckled, stroking his beard. "Your *anvil-shaped* heart." Then he said, "Anyhow, let me handle this. Fire is the purview of my people!" And he stuck the cheese on the skewers and put them over the fire. He roasted them with quick, sure movements like a wizard casting a spell. A sweet scent mixed with the rising smoke.

Before they knew it, the cheese began to melt and run. The dwarf passed the skewers to his fellow adventurers, and they each brought it to their mouths.

"It is sweet, like nectar!"

Lizard Priest gave an ecstatic shout and thumped his tail on the ground. "Like nectar, it is!"

"Glad the first cheese of your life didn't disappoint," the dwarf said, taking a big bite of his own slice and washing it down with a gulp of fire wine. "Ahh, fire wine and cheese, there's a fine pairing!"

He dabbed at the wine that he dribbled into his beard and gave a contented sigh. The elf frowned. Seeming quite back to her normal, haughty self, she took dainty bites of her cheese.

"Hmm. It's kind of sour but…sweet," she said. "Sort of like a banana." Her long ears made a wide motion up and down. Then her eyes narrowed like a cat's when coughing up a hairball.

"Is this from that farm?" Priestess asked with a bright smile, halfway through her own piece of cheese.

"It is."

"It's delicious!"

"Is it?"

Goblin Slayer nodded quietly and calmly put a piece of cheese into his mouth. He chewed, swallowed, took a mouthful of fire wine, and then pulled his bag closer. The next day they would enter the goblins' nest. He had to double-check his gear.

The bag was packed with a variety of bottles, ropes, chains, and unidentifiable items. The elf, whose stupor had been cleared away by the sharp, sweet cheese, looked at the collection with interest.

Goblin Slayer was examining a scroll that was tied shut in a peculiar way. The elf reached out just as, seemingly satisfied with the knots, Goblin Slayer was putting the scroll back into his bag.

"Don't touch that," he said flatly. The elf drew her hand back hastily. "It's dangerous."

"I-I wasn't going to touch it. I was just looking."

"Don't look at it. It's dangerous."

The elf gave a little sneer in his direction. Goblin Slayer was unperturbed.

Unwilling to take no for an answer, the elf glanced at the scroll out of the corner of her eye. "Isn't that a magic scroll?" she asked. "I've never seen one before."

At her words, not just Priestess but the dwarf and the lizardman leaned in for a look.

A magic scroll. An item sometimes found in ancient ruins, albeit very rarely. Unroll it, and even an infant could cast the spell written there. The knowledge of how to make them was long lost, even to the oldest of the high elves. Magical items were rare enough, but such scrolls were among the rarest of all.

But for all that, they were surprisingly inconvenient items for adventurers. Any of an infinite variety of spells might be written on them, from the most useful to the most mundane, and they could be used only once, anyway. Many adventurers simply sold them—for a tidy sum—to researchers or collectors of curio. A wizard in the party was magic enough for them. They needed money more than scrolls.

Goblin Slayer was one of the few who had kept his scroll. Even Priestess hadn't known he had it.

"All right, all right. I won't touch, I won't even look, but will you at least tell us what spell is written on it?"

"No." He didn't so much as look at her. "If you were captured and told the goblins, then what? You'll know what it is when I use it."

"…You don't like me, do you?"

"I'm not particular."

"Isn't that just a way of saying you don't care?"

"I mean no more than I said."

The elf gritted her teeth, and her ears flapped angrily.

"Give it up, long-ears. He's stubborner than I am." The dwarf laughed happily. "He's Beard-cutter, after all."

"You mean Orcbolg."

"I am Goblin Slayer," he muttered.

The elf frowned at this, and the dwarf stroked his beard in amusement.

"Um, excuse me," Priestess broke in, "but what does *Orcbolg* mean, exactly?"

"It's the name of a sword that appears in our legends," the elf said. She held up a finger proudly like a teacher instructing her pupils. "It was a goblin-slaying blade that would glow blue when an *orc*—a goblin—was near."

"Let it be said, though, that it was we dwarves who forged it," Dwarf Shaman interjected.

The elf snorted. "And called it 'Beard-cutter.' What an awful name. Dwarves might have good heads for crafting, but not for anything else."

"So, long-ears, you admit that your people aren't the skilled craftsmen mine are!" He heaved a huge belly laugh. The elf puffed out her cheeks.

The lizardman gave a great roll of his eyes, as if he couldn't believe what he was seeing, and exchanged a look with Priestess. She was beginning to understand that this was his way of making a joke.

She had come to appreciate the friendly arguments, too. It was just how elves and dwarves were. Priestess, faced for the first time with people of other races, knew she could never trust her party members if she didn't get to know them. So she went out of her way to talk with them, and in no time at all, they had become fast friends.

The lizardman's ancestral faith did not clash with the teachings of the all-compassionate Earth Mother. And there was another girl in the party who was Priestess's age—or who at least looked it. It put her very much at ease.

Goblin Slayer, for his part, didn't seem to especially embrace or reject any of them. But this seemed somehow quite to the dwarf's liking. Whatever Goblin Slayer did that annoyed the elf, he seemed to enjoy imitating it.

This strange little party had met most unexpectedly, and yet, somehow, there was a sense they belonged together.

Priestess felt an unusual warmth spreading through her.

"Hey, wanna go adventuring with us?"

Which wasn't to say there was nothing that pricked at her heart…

"Oh yes, there is a thing I have been wondering," the lizardman said, his tail sounding, opening his jaw. The fire danced. Before he asked his question, he made the strange, palms-together gesture. He claimed it was an expression of gratitude for the meal.

"Wherefrom do the goblins spring? My grandfather once told me of a kingdom under the earth…"

"I"—the dwarf burped—"heard that they were fallen rheas or elves."

"What prejudice!" High Elf Archer glared at Dwarf Shaman. "*I* was taught goblins are what become of dwarves who grow obsessed with gold."

"Prejudice, indeed!" The dwarf looked triumphantly at the elf, who shook her head slightly.

"Now, now, didn't our priest say they came from under the earth? And isn't that where dwarves come from?"

"Grrr…!" The dwarf could only grit his teeth at this. The elf gave a satisfied chuckle. The lizardman, of course, licked his nose with his tongue.

"Under the earth I said, but of elves or dwarves naught. What stories do humans tell, Priestess?"

"Oh, um…" Priestess had been in the midst of gathering everyone's dinnerware and wiping it clean. She set the work aside and straightened, putting her hands on her knees. "We have a saying that when someone fails at something, a goblin appears."

"What?!" The elf giggled.

Priestess nodded with a smile. "It's just a way of teaching manners. *If you don't do such and such, a goblin will come for you!*"

"That seems grim news indeed, girl!" the dwarf said. "Why, long-ears alone would account for an entire goblin army!"

"Hey!" The elf's ears pointed straight back. "How rude. Just wait till tomorrow. You'll see if any of my arrows fail to hit their target."

"Oh, they'll hit something, all right—I'm afraid they'll hit me, right in the back!"

"Fine. Little dwarves are welcome to hide behind me."

"Damn right I will! You're a ranger, aren't you? A little scouting would help us all out," the dwarf said, patting his beard with a smirk.

The elf raised her arm and seemed about to reply, when a single, muttered word dropped between them. "I…"

Naturally, the group's attention turned toward the source.

"I heard they come from the moon," Goblin Slayer said.

"By 'the moon,' do you refer to one of the two in our sky?" the lizardman asked.

"Yes." Goblin Slayer nodded. "The green one. Green rocks, green monsters."

"Well, never thought they might've come from over my head," the dwarf said with a long, thoughtful sigh.

With great interest, the elf asked, "So, shooting stars are goblins coming down here?"

"Don't know. But there is no grass, or trees, or water on the moon. Only rocks. It's a lonely place," he said soberly. "They don't like it there. They want somewhere better. They're envious of us, jealous, so they come down here."

"Here?"

"Yes." He nodded. "So when you get jealous, you become like a goblin."

"I get it," the elf said with a disappointed breath. "Another little story to teach kids manners."

"Um, who told you that story?" Priestess asked, leaning forward slightly. He was always so realistic and rational. This kind of tale seemed unlike him.

"My older sister."

"Oh, you have an older sister?"

He nodded. "Had."

Priestess giggled softly. The thought of this hardened adventurer being scolded by his sister was somehow heartening.

"So," the elf pressed, "you really believe goblins come from the moon?"

Goblin Slayer nodded slightly.

"All I know," he said, staring up at the twin orbs in the sky, "is that my sister was never wrong. About anything."

With that, he fell silent. The bonfire crackled. With her long ears, the elf detected the hint of a sigh.

She quietly moved her face closer to Goblin Slayer's helmet. She still couldn't make out his expression. A mischievous grin spread across her face. "Pfft. He fell asleep!"

"Oh-ho, fire wine finally got to him, did it?" The dwarf was just shaking the last drop from the bottle.

"Come to think of it, he's had his fair share of that stuff, hasn't he?"

Priestess took a blanket from their gear and carefully placed it over him. Ever so gently, she touched the leather armor on his chest. She was tired, too, but he needed to rest.

"Let us, too, take our repose," the lizardman said solemnly. "And let us determine the watch. A good night's sleep will itself be a weapon in our arsenal."

Priestess, the elf, and the dwarf each volunteered for a shift.

As she snuggled down under her blanket, the elf stole a glance at Goblin Slayer. "Hmm," she murmured to herself. "They say a wild animal never sleeps in front of those it doesn't trust…"

To her own annoyance, she found this inspired in her a faint glow of happiness.

Goblin

Orc in elvish.
Be careful of pronunciation.

[CHARACTERISTICS]

Goblins possess the size and physique of human
children; their personalities and behavior are like
children's but with an extra dose of capriciousness
and cruelty. Individually they are not very threatening
and are considered the weakest of monsters. They
often attack human settlements seeking plunder
and to abduct local women, using them for
breeding. They are numerous.

← Important: Small parties of
Porcelain ranks and women should
be advised to hunt giant rats in
the sewers instead.

Pulled from reports by some adventurers;
requires confirmation.

← More like
"reports by *him*."

[LIFESTYLE]

Goblins primarily live in caves. They are excellent
scavengers and quick learners. Tribal structure
consists of males only. Their lifestyle is similar
to that of Paleolithic man. They lack a unique
culture of their own. Everything they need, they
steal. There are a wide variety of subspecies,
including Shamans, Riders (cavalry), and hobgoblins.
When goblins breed with other races, it always
results in a goblin child.

Case No. 0506:
Party wiped, request relief personnel.

↑ Again? I'm not sure
we should be expecting
him to handle things
every single time.

CHAPTER 7

GOBLIN SLAYER

The nest was smack in the middle of a huge field.

Maybe *nest* wasn't even the right word for it. It had a square entrance of white stone that jutted up from the ground, half-buried in the earth. This was no cave. It was clearly man-made: ancient ruins.

The pale stone caught the light of the fading sun, shimmering red as blood.

Two goblins stood guard. They were stationed on either side of the entranceway, spears in their hands, poor leather plate covering their bodies. With them was a dog—no, a wolf.

"GURUU…"

"GAU!"

One of the goblins, glancing around, made to sit down and was scolded by the other. The first monster forced himself to stand, yawned widely, and looked at the sun with undisguised hatred, The wolf lay on the ground beside them. Its ears twitched. Wild animals didn't let down their guard even when they rested.

The elf saw all this from the bushes not far away.

"Goblins with a guard dog? You've got to be kidding me."

"It proves this horde has time and resources to spare." Next to her, Goblin Slayer lay prone on the ground. He was tying a bit of rope to a small rock, his gaze never straying from the goblins. "Stay alert. There must be a lot of them inside."

"Just out of curiosity, what if the horde didn't have extra resources?"

"Then they wouldn't keep the dog. They'd eat it."

The elf shook her head. She shouldn't have asked. Lizard Priest laughed soundlessly.

"Is this safe?" the elf asked. "It's going to be night soon. Shouldn't we wait, make our move during the day tomorrow?"

"It's early morning for them now. The time is right."

"...Fine, then. Here goes."

The elf drew an arrow like she drew breath.

The elves did not use iron. The shafts of their arrows were made of tree branches that naturally had the right size and shape; the heads were animal teeth, and for the feathers, they used leaves.

High Elf Archer's bow, made of the branch of a great beech tree and strung with spider's silk, was taller than she was. But she handled it lightly, crouching in the underbrush and fitting an arrow to the string.

The spider's silk made a sibilant sound as she pulled it tight.

"Tell me those things work better than they look," the dwarf said despairingly. He found he couldn't trust a bit of wood and leaves. "Please don't miss! You have a quiver full of arrows, but we've got only so many spells."

"Hush," the elf commanded archly. The dwarf obediently shut his mouth. After that, no one said anything.

The bow bent with the merest sound of straining wood. The wind whistled. The elf moved her long ears ever so slightly.

The goblin on the right yawned. The elf loosed her arrow.

It left her bow soundlessly. But it appeared to have landed several paces to the right of the goblins.

Dwarf Shaman gave a frank cluck of his tongue. The elf, though, was smiling. She already had a second arrow in her hand.

In an instant, the grounded arrow drew a large arc through the air, passing through the goblin on the right and taking part of his spine with it. It continued into the cheek of the goblin on the left; it encountered his eye socket and drove straight through.

The wolf leaped up, not sure what had happened but opening its mouth to howl a warning—

"Too late!"

The elf loosed the second arrow almost too quickly to see. The wolf flew back. It was only then that the two goblins collapsed to the ground like twin sacks of bricks, dead.

It was a spectacular display of skill, far beyond human capacity.

"That was amazing!" Priestess looked admiringly at the elf.

"Indeed," Lizard Priest said, his large eyes growing even larger. "But what did you do? Is it some kind of sorcery?"

The elf gave a proud chuckle and shook her head. "Any sufficiently advanced technology is indistinguishable from magic." Her ears bobbed knowingly.

"That's a bold statement with me standing here," said Dwarf Shaman, who was quite well versed in both technology and magic.

"Two... Strange." Goblin Slayer stood up from the bushes. When the elf's arrow missed, he had been planning to fling his rock at the enemy instead.

"What? Got a problem?" the elf said, thinking he was referring to her archery.

He shook his head with a hint of exasperation. "They were afraid. Have you ever known a diligent goblin?"

"You don't think they're worried because they're next door to an elf forest?"

"We can hope," he said, and with that halfhearted answer, he strode over to the goblins and knelt down to inspect their corpses.

"Oh, um..." Priestess seemed to guess what he was doing. "Sh-shall I h-help...?" she asked in a thin voice, a stiff smile on her face.

"No need," Goblin Slayer said bluntly. Priestess let out a sigh of relief. Her face had gone a bit pale.

"What are you doing?" The elf, whose curiosity was naturally piqued by this exchange, walked over to Goblin Slayer and looked down.

A knife had appeared in his hand. He dug it into the goblin's corpse and casually cut out the creature's guts.

The elf stiffened and tugged at his arm. "H-how can you do that to them? I know you hate goblins, but you don't have to—"

"They have an excellent sense of smell."

"...Huh?"

Goblin Slayer was calm as he delivered this answer that was no answer. He daubed his gauntlets with blood, then pulled a liver out from one of the bodies.

"Especially for the scent of women, children, and elves."

"Wa…wait a second. Orcbolg. You can't possibly mean…"

In reply, Goblin Slayer wrapped the liver in a hand cloth and squeezed.

High Elf Archer, finally understanding where he got the stains on his armor, went whiter than the stones that towered over them.

§

Moments later, the dead guards hidden safely in the bushes, the party advanced toward the ruins. The chalky walls surrounded a narrow pathway that seemed to slope gently downward.

Goblin Slayer was in the lead. With his sword he tapped the floor and walls. Then he tossed his pet rock forward, saw that it landed safely, and reeled it back in.

"No traps."

"Hmm. I speculate, but this place appears to be a temple."

"It looks like this field was the site of a battle back during the Age of the Gods," Priestess said. She brushed her hand across a carving in the wall. "Maybe it's a fortress or something from back then… Although the construction certainly seems human…"

"First a home for soldiers, now for goblins. Which is crueler?" Lizard Priest pondered grimly, joining his hands.

"Speaking of cruel," the dwarf chimed in, "are you going to be all right, long-ears?"

"Errgh… I think I'm gonna be sick," High Elf Archer whimpered. Her traditional hunting gear was covered in gore. The liquid that had come spurting out of the goblin's liver coated her hair and ran down her body. Even the dwarf lacked the heart to tease her in this state.

"Get used to it," Goblin Slayer said from next to the elf. On his left, his shield was fixed to his arm, and in his hand was a torch. In his right hand, his sword glinted. The elf shot him a glare as she changed her great bow for a smaller one, but the tears held back in the corners of her eyes and the pitiful droop of her ears made her less than intimidating.

"When we get back, I hope you remember this!"

"I'll remember," he said shortly.

The torch guttered. The elves' wards seemed to extend even here. Or perhaps, many, many moons ago, the elves had lived on this land.

To Goblin Slayer, the real problem was that this limited his ability to attack with fire.

"You humans are downright inconvenient," the dwarf said, patting his mustache. Of the party members, Goblin Slayer alone carried a torch. The dwarf, elf, and lizardman all had varying degrees of night vision.

"I know. That's why we have our tricks."

"Well, I wish you'd think of some better ones," High Elf Archer said dejectedly.

Priestess, feeling quite sorry for her, spoke up in an attempt to offer some comfort. "Um, it'll come out when you wash...mostly."

"You understand my pain."

"I'm used to it," she said with a weak smile. Her vestments were, once again, covered in goblin juices. Priestess stood in the middle of their formation, lightly gripping her sounding staff. The path was wide enough for two to walk abreast, so High Elf Archer and Goblin Slayer went side by side in front of Priestess, while Dwarf Shaman and Lizard Priest came behind. She was Porcelain-ranked, after all. She was the weakest and most fragile member of their party. They had to protect her.

Despite this, and despite Priestess's touch of an inferiority complex, none of the others saw her as a burden. Every spell caster could use only so many spells, so many times. None of them were Platinum-ranked adventurers who could use their magic or miracles dozens of times a day. Having a healer in the group might mean someone had a spell left when it was needed most.

Or rather, one who could conserve their spells was one who could survive...

Priestess watched her companions in attentive silence. She held her staff loosely.

It's almost like any other adventure...

And suddenly, she was walking in front of Wizard again.

Just like that first time...

With trembling lips, Priestess recited the name of the Earth Mother several times. She hoped nothing would happen on this quest. But she knew it was a futile wish.

The adventurers' footsteps echoed weirdly from the pavestones on the path. There was no sign of goblins. Yet.

"The underground and I are old friends, but I don't like it here," the dwarf said, wiping sweat from his forehead. They had been proceeding on a slight downward diagonal since they entered the ruins. The path looked straight to the naked eye, but actually curved very slowly, forming a corkscrew. The turning and the descending played havoc with the adventurers' sense of balance.

"It almost seems like we're in a tower," Priestess said, exhaling.

"Some of the old fortresses were indeed built in such a shape," the lizardman said. At the rear end of the party, his tail swung back and forth.

"I wish we could've come here when it *wasn't* infested with goblins," the elf whispered. "I would've liked to look around a little."

Sometime later, the slope ended and the path split off left and right. Both routes looked identical.

"Wait," the elf said sharply.

"What is it?"

"Don't move," she said to Goblin Slayer.

She crawled along the ground. Her fingers reached into the space between the paving stones just ahead of them, seeking something.

"An alarm?" he asked.

"Probably. I noticed it because it's brand-new, but it would have been easy to miss. Everyone be careful."

The spot the elf indicated was indeed raised a little. Step on it, and a noisemaker would sound somewhere, alerting the goblins to the intruders.

Priestess swallowed heavily. The long, twisting slope had thrown off her concentration and her senses. She could see the trap now that it had been pointed out to her, but without the elf's warning, she would surely have missed it.

"Goblins. Impudent beasts," the dwarf spat, patting his beard.

Wordlessly, Goblin Slayer cast the torchlight on the floor, then down each of the passageways left and right, looking closely at the walls. There was nothing there, save for the soot of the lamps once used by the fortress's long-vanished residents.

"What's wrong?" Priestess asked.

"No totems."

"Oh, you're right..." Only Priestess understood Goblin Slayer's remark. The other party members listened in puzzlement. But Goblin Slayer said nothing more.

He's thinking. Priestess looked at the party and realized it fell to her to explain.

"Um, in other words, that means there's no, um, goblin shamans here."

"No spell caster?" the elf said with a happy clap. "Lucky us."

"No."

The lizardman let out a hissing breath. "Are you, then...troubled by the absence of spell casters, milord Goblin Slayer?"

"Yes." He nodded, then indicated the alarm with the tip of his sword. "Your average goblin would never come up with something like this."

"Long-ears said it was brand-new. That means it's not part of the fort's original defenses."

"I thought about tripping it to draw them out," Goblin Slayer muttered. "But I think we had better not."

"Milord Goblin Slayer, you spoke before of your experience with such extensive nests," the lizardman said, taking care that his tail did not drag across the alarm. "How did you deal with them?"

"I flushed out the inhabitants and annihilated them one at a time. Sometimes I used fire. Sometimes I directed a river into the nest. There are various ways." Standing next to him, the elf looked aghast. "But we can't use those here." He turned to High Elf Archer. "Can you make out any footprints?"

"I'm sorry. In a cave, maybe, but on stone like this..."

"Let the dwarf have a look," Dwarf Shaman said, coming over.

"Fine, but watch out for the alarm."

"I'm stout, not stupid. I'll be careful."

The elf politely made way. He stooped in front of the party. He walked back and forth across the bar of the T-shaped intersection. He kicked the stone floor, looking at it intently. A moment later, he gave his beard a confident stroke. "I see it. Their little roost is to the left."

Priestess was confused. "How can you tell?"

"By the wear on the floor. They're coming from the left and returning from the right, or coming from the left and turning to go outside."

"Are you sure?" Goblin Slayer said.

"Of course I'm sure. I'm a dwarf," Dwarf Shaman replied, pounding his belly.

"I see," Goblin Slayer murmured, falling silent.

"Is something wrong, milord Goblin Slayer?" the lizardman said.

"We'll go this way," Goblin Slayer said, and with his sword, he pointed...to the right.

"Didn't Stumpy just say the goblins are to the left?" the elf said.

"Yes. But if we go that way, we'll be too late."

"Too late for what?"

"You'll see," he said with a calm nod.

Not long after starting down the rightward path, they were assaulted by a choking stench. The air was thick and cloying. An acrid taste lingered in their mouths with every breath.

"Hrk..." The dwarf pinched his nose.

"Urgh..." The lizardman's eyes rolled grimly in his head.

The elf, too, unconsciously took a hand from her bow and covered her mouth.

"Wha...what *is* that? Is it safe to breathe?" she groaned.

Priestess's teeth were chattering. She knew this smell.

"Don't fight it. Breathe through your nose. You'll get used to it soon." Goblin Slayer didn't look back but only walked resolutely farther down the passage.

The party hurried to keep up. Even Priestess somehow managed to continue.

The source of the stench was close. They came up against a rotting wooden door that seemed placed to section off part of the ruins.

"Hmph." Goblin Slayer gave it a solid kick. With an agonized creak, the door abandoned its duty and collapsed. The foul liquid that covered the floor splashed up as the door fell into it.

This was where the goblins put every manner of refuse. Scraps of food, including bones with bits of flesh clinging to them. Excrement. Corpses. Everything. The formerly white walls had turned a grimy crimson with the piles of trash.

Amid it all, they could make out a strand of flaxen hair and a leg attached to a chain. Four wasted limbs bore hideous scars. The tendons had been cut.

It was an elf.

Emaciated, buried in filth, the left half of her body nonetheless still showed the beauty her people were renowned for.

The right half was a different story.

Priestess thought the elf looked like she had been covered in bunches of grapes. Her delicate, pale skin was invisible under bluish swelling. Her eye and her breast were wrecked.

The goal was unmistakable: torture for torture's sake.

Oh, not again… The thought rose in Priestess's mind and stuck there.

"Huegh… Eurghhh…"

Right next to Priestess—seemingly so far away—High Elf Archer was adding the contents of her stomach to the waste that covered the floor.

"What *is* this?" The dwarf stroked his beard, but couldn't conceal the horror on his face.

"Milord Goblin Slayer?" Even the normally inscrutable Lizard Priest wore an expression of transparent disgust.

"You've never seen this before?"

At his quiet question, High Elf Archer nodded, not bothering to wipe her mouth. Tears dribbled down her cheeks, and her ears hung almost flat against her head.

"I see." He nodded.

"…illl… …ki… killll…" Priestess looked up suddenly at the plaintive groan. The imprisoned elf. She was still alive! Priestess rushed over to her and held her up, ignoring the filth that immediately covered her hands.

"Give me a potion!"

"No, she is too much weakened. It will only catch in her throat." The lizardman had followed Priestess over to the prisoner and was inspecting her wounds with his scaled claws. "She is not wounded fatally, but she is in peril of dying from exhaustion. She needs a miracle."

"Right!" Priestess drew her staff close to her chest with one hand and placed the other on the chest of the wounded elf. "*O Earth Mother, abounding in mercy, lay your revered hand upon your child's wounds.*"

Watching their healer bestow the goddess's miracle out of the corner of his eye, Goblin Slayer approached High Elf Archer.

"Do you know her?"

Still crouched and shaking helplessly, the elf shook her head. "Most...most likely she was like me...a 'rootless' elf who...became an adventurer."

"I see." Goblin Slayer nodded and then with his bold stride walked toward the prisoner. His sword was in his hand. The lizardman gave him a wary look.

"Oh...!"

We're out of time.

Priestess blanched and rose. "H-hold it right there!" She stood with her arms spread in front of the prostrate elf. Goblin Slayer did not stop.

"Move."

"No! I...I won't!"

"I don't know what illusion you're harboring now," Goblin Slayer said in exasperation. His tone didn't change. It was merciless, calm. "But I came here for one purpose: to slay goblins."

His sword fell.

There was a geyser of blood and a scream.

"Three."

The thud of a body. It was a goblin, the sword through his brain. He dropped the poisoned dagger he had been holding as he died. No one had noticed him hiding in the pile of trash behind the imprisoned elf.

No, Priestess thought, shaking her head. That wasn't true. *He* had noticed. And the prisoner, too.

"Ki...kill them...all..." The elf adventurer brought up a mouthful of blood along with her words.

Goblin Slayer set his foot against the corpse and pulled out his sword. He used the goblin's tunic to wipe glittering fat off the blade.

"That's my intention," he answered calmly. No one else said anything.

What had this man seen in his life? What was he? The people standing in that filth-riddled room finally felt a glimmer of understanding.

Priestess recalled Witch's appraisal of Goblin Slayer. And her words: "*Let it be, your own decision.*"

Now she understood clearly what that meant. Every adventurer, even those who didn't survive their first quest, would experience killing and death. They would encounter awful and terrible things. Villages and cities ravaged by monsters would not be an unusual sight for them.

But there was a logic behind it all. From bandits and hoodlums, to dark elves and dragons, even slimes—all had a reason for how they acted.

Goblins alone were different. They had no reason. Only evil. Evil toward humans, toward every other living thing. To hunt goblins was to be confronted with that evil over and over again.

That was no adventure. And someone who chose to go down that path—they were no adventurer. They were *him.*

A man in grimy leather armor and a dirty helmet, carrying a sword that seemed almost too long to wield.

"Goblin Slayer…"

Amid the dark and the stench, someone whispered his name.

CHAPTER 8

Goblin Slaying

The responsibility to provide an escort for the elf prisoner back to the forest fell to Lizard Priest.

He took several small fangs out of his pouch and spread them on the floor.

"*O horns and claws of our father, Iguanodon,*" he intoned, "*thy four limbs, become two legs to walk upon the earth.*"

When he had spoken, the fangs on the ground clattered and began to swell in size. A moment later, they had formed the skeleton of a lizard-man, who bowed its head to Lizard Priest and kneeled.

"This is the Dragontooth Warrior, a miracle I received from my father," he explained.

"How well does it fight?" Goblin Slayer asked.

"As I myself am fairly capable, it could deal with one or two goblins if the need arose."

The lizardman wrote a letter explaining the situation and gave it to the Dragontooth Warrior, after which the creature hoisted the elf over its shoulder and set off.

Between this and Minor Heal, the party had now used two of its miracles. No one objected.

"What the hell...? What is going *on* here?" High Elf Archer whimpered, crouched in the muck. Priestess patted her back.

Strangely, although they were still in the filth-riddled room, they no longer noticed the smell.

I guess we must have gotten used to it.

Priestess gave a rueful smile. Her arms and legs trembled just a little.

Dwarf Shaman was tugging roughly at his beard and scowling. Claiming he felt unwell, he had gone to stand in the doorway of the room. The Dragontooth Warrior, with its elf load, passed by him.

Goblin Slayer had his back turned to it all. He rummaged through the mess, pushing things around, tossing them aside, until at last he pulled something out of the garbage.

It was a canvas knapsack, clearly meant for an adventurer. Goblins had clawed at the inside but had thrown it away. Perhaps they had tired of it. It was awfully dirty. Goblin Slayer, too, began to paw through it.

"Ah, I knew it had to be here." He took out a balled-up scrap of paper, yellow with age.

"What's that?" Priestess asked softly, as she patted the elf on the back.

"It must have belonged to that prisoner," Goblin Slayer said, calmly unballing the paper—no, it was a dried leaf. With his finger he traced the flowing lines that had been drawn on it, then nodded as if he had found what he wanted.

"It's a map of these ruins."

"That elf must have been using it to navigate…" There was a good chance that, unhappily, she had not known the ruins had become a goblin nest. Insofar as heading into some abandoned ruins was an adventure, the fate she'd suffered was certainly one possible outcome.

That they had been in time to save her was sheer dumb luck. As much as Priestess hated to admit it.

"The left path leads to a gallery," Goblin Slayer said, studying the map intently, "which borders an atrium. I can almost guarantee most of the horde is there. It's the only place large enough for them all to sleep." He folded the map and put it into his own bag. "It seems left was the correct choice."

"Hmph." The dwarf gave an affronted snort.

Goblin Slayer also took a few bottles of ointment and other small items from the knapsack.

And then, without preamble, he flung the bag at High Elf Archer. She was bewildered.

"You take it."

As High Elf Archer put on the knapsack, she looked up. The corners of her eyes were red and puffy from her rubbing them; she looked very uncomfortable.

"Let's go."

"Now hold on, you can't talk like that to—"

"It's all right." The elf cut off Priestess's indignant tirade.

"We...we have to hurry."

"That's right," Goblin Slayer said calmly. "We have to kill those goblins." He walked with his usual bold, somehow violent stride. Over the collapsed door he went, leaving the room full of trash behind.

He didn't look back.

"H-hey, wait up—!"

The elf called out and rushed to follow him while Priestess went along in silence.

The remaining two adventurers looked at each other.

"...Gods above," the dwarf sighed, twisting his beard. "He's a real piece of work, that one. I wonder if he's even human."

"I have heard Eotyrannus, the Dawn Tyrant, was also thus. It seems the stories are not altogether untrue." The lizardman gave a wide roll of his eyes.

"Maybe you have to be a little crazy to be good at this job."

"Be that as it may, we must go. I, for my part, cannot forgive those creatures."

"Nor I, Scaly. Goblins are the age-old enemies of the dwarves, when you get right down to it."

Dwarf Shaman and Lizard Priest looked at each other, then went after Goblin Slayer.

The leftward path twisted like a maze. It was only natural for a fortress. If you didn't know the lay of the land, you would never figure it out.

But they had the map left by the elf and two people watching carefully for traps. They did encounter several goblin patrols on their way through the fortress, but it was nothing unexpected. High Elf Archer fired her arrows into them from her short bow, and if this failed to stop them, Goblin Slayer would leap into the fray and finish them off.

In the end, not a single goblin survived its encounter with the party.

Priestess looked discreetly at the elf's face, taut like a drawn bowstring.

She had seen the elf's almost miraculous shooting at the entrance to the ruins. The idea that her arrows could ever fail to stop their targets seemed almost unfathomable...

Goblin Slayer, though, did not seem bothered. He forged ahead with the same calm stride as always.

Finally, they reached the last place to take a rest before the gallery.

"How much magic do we have left?" Goblin Slayer asked quietly. He stayed close to the wall, changing out his own weapon.

High Elf Archer was crouched in the corner, and Priestess moved to stand near her, offering a pat on the shoulder. "Um, I used Minor Heal once already, so...I have two miracles left," she said.

"I have called upon a Dragontooth Warrior only once," the lizardman said. "I, too, can use up to three miracles, but..." His tail swishing back and forth, he reached into his bag and brought out a handful of teeth. "The miracle of the Dragontooth Warrior requires a material component. I can perform it perhaps one more time only."

"I understand." Goblin Slayer nodded. His gaze fell on the dwarf. "What about you?"

"Well, let's see..." The dwarf began to count on his small fingers, muttering "one, two..." under his breath. "It depends on the spell," he concluded, "but say four times, maybe five. Well, four for certain. Don't worry."

"I see."

The number of times a spell caster could use their magics increased with their rank—but not dramatically. Spell casters' real power lay in the variety and difficulty of the spells they could cast. If they were not a Platinum-ranked adventurer—and even then, one with a remarkable gift—the number of times they could cast per day was limited.

It meant every spell was precious. Waste them and die.

"Um, would you like a drink? Can you drink?"

"Thanks." High Elf Archer took the canteen Priestess offered her and put it to her lips.

She had been all but silent until this point. The elf had always received Priestess's concerns with the faintest smile and a shake of the head.

Who could blame her? Priestess thought. *After seeing what became of another elf like that...*

Priestess herself sometimes dreamed of what had happened to her former companions.

At the time, she and Goblin Slayer had taken one quest after another almost without pause. Looking back on it, she was glad she had not had time to stop and think.

"Don't put too much in your stomach. It will slow your blood flow," Goblin Slayer said calmly. "You won't react as quickly."

He wasn't saying it for the elf's benefit. It was just a practicality. He was making sure they were all aware.

Priestess stood, as if unconsciously covering the elf. "Goblin Slayer, sir!" she said. "Can't you be...a little more...?"

"I don't want to mislead anyone," he said with a slow shake of his head. "If you are able to join me, then join me. If you aren't, then go back. It's that simple."

"...Don't be ridiculous," the elf said, wiping drops of water from her mouth. "I'm a ranger. Orcbolg...you, even you, couldn't handle scouting and looking for traps and fighting all by yourself."

"Those who can should do what they are able."

"I'm saying we don't have the strength. There's only five of us."

"Numbers are not the issue. It would be much worse to leave this place be."

"Oh, for the gods' sake!" The elf tore at her hair. Her ears pointed straight back. "What is *happening* here? I don't even know anymore..."

"...Will you go back, then?"

"How can I?! After seeing what they did to that prisoner?! And my home... My home isn't so far away from here..."

"I see" was his only response to the agitated archer. "In that case, let's go." With that, he stood, announcing the end of their brief respite.

Goblin Slayer went ahead without another word. The elf stared daggers at his back, grinding her teeth.

"Calm down, long-ears. Enemy territory is not the place to start a fight."

There was a pause. "You're right," the elf said.

The dwarf patted her gently on the back. The elf's long ears drooped.

"I'm sorry. I do hate to agree with a dwarf. Even when he's right."

"Ah, there's the long-ears I know!"

Short bow in hand, the elf walked off. Priestess gave the dwarf a small bow as she went by. The dwarf followed, digging in his pack. And the lizardman once again made up the tail of their line.

"Can't be too careful," the dwarf said.

"Indeed. I ought to make preparations to pray." The lizardman made his strange palms-together gesture.

§

Following the map, the party soon found the gallery.

The elf went in front, raised up on her tiptoes like a stalking cat. She gestured to the others how to proceed.

Hence she was the first to see the vast hall.

Just as the map showed, the gallery ran along the edge of a huge atrium. The ceiling had to be as high as ground level. Elves lived for thousands of years, and there could hardly have been a forest dweller as old as this room.

Despite their age, the white stone walls still bore striking illustrations of the battles from the Age of the Gods. The beautiful gods fought with the terrible ones, swords flashing, lightning bolts flying, until finally they reached for the dice.

It was a depiction of the creation of the world. If this place had once been a fortress, what must the soldiers here have felt upon seeing this? If the circumstances had been different, High Elf Archer would have let out an entranced sigh.

But the circumstances were not different, and she kept her mouth shut.

She leaned over the railing of the gallery and peered out into the atrium. By a wall that rose sheer as a cliff, she could see goblins.

And not one or two. Not even ten or twenty.

A vast host. Five adventurers could not have counted the number on their collective fingers.

The elf swallowed. The smoldering rage in her chest went suddenly cold.

That prisoner might have been made the plaything of every goblin in this room. The elf suddenly registered what might happen to her with the slightest slip.

She didn't have the courage to face this alone. She bit her lip to stop her teeth from chattering.

"How is it?"

The elf nearly jumped in surprise. Her ears flew back.

How had Goblin Slayer come up beside her without her noticing?

Partly, the elf had been focused on other things. But Goblin Slayer moved now with a delicacy she could never have guessed from his usual violent gait. He didn't make a sound.

He was not holding a torch, perhaps out of concern it might be seen.

"D-don't scare me like that…"

"I didn't mean to."

The elf glared angrily at the steel helmet. She wiped the sweat that had appeared on her forehead.

"Anyway, see for yourself. There's a lot of them."

"It won't be a problem," Goblin Slayer said calmly.

He gestured to the other party members to join them, then quickly explained his plan.

No one argued.

§

The first to notice something unusual was a goblin who had crawled out of bed. It was almost time to change the guard, but the last patrol hadn't come back yet.

Well, maybe he'd go torment that elf a little more. True, it wasn't as much fun now that her screams were growing weaker. Hopefully, they would catch another one soon.

Unbeknownst to him, an opportunity to do just that was coming his way.

The goblin gave a long stretch, loosening his thin frame and letting his bulging belly hang. Just as his stretch turned into a yawn, he saw something strange perched upon the gallery.

A dwarf.

A dwarf downing the contents of a red jar.

"GUI...?"

At that moment, the dwarf looked down at the bewildered goblin and spat at him. The spit came down in a mist.

The goblin sneezed. This was liquor! That dwarf had spit alcohol on him!

"Drink deep, sing loud, let the spirits lead you! Sing loud, step quick, and when you sleep they see you, may a jar of fire wine be in your dreams to greet you!" And then, once more, the dwarf let a few drops of his drink dribble down on the befuddled monster.

The goblin was thoroughly perplexed by all this, but he knew enough to alert his companions. He opened his mouth and...

...didn't make a sound.

His tongue moved and he drew breath, but his voice didn't come out.

Now, why do you suppose that was?

Looking closely, the goblin could see a gorgeous human girl standing next to the dwarf, waving a sounding staff.

"O Earth Mother, abounding in mercy, grant us peace to accept all things..."

The goblin did not seem to grasp the words the thin voice was saying. The rusty gears in his little head turned as fast as they could, but somehow he felt floaty and kind of...nice.

The last patrol hadn't come back yet. Why not catch another few winks until they did?

He gave a great yawn and climbed back into bed.

And then he died.

He never knew he had been the victim of Silence and Stupor. Goblin Slayer cut his throat with a dagger before he ever had the chance to find out. The goblin opened his eyes, blood bubbling up at the wound, but Goblin Slayer pressed the dagger home and killed him.

High Elf Archer and Lizard Priest came down from the gallery without a sound and put their weapons to work all through the great hall. They had to move quickly in order to finish the job while the spells cast by Priestess and the dwarf were still active.

They had to be calm, ruthless. Cut the throat of a sleeping goblin, crush it down until he stopped moving, then go on to the next one. It wasn't a battle. It was just work.

But not easy work. The elf made a voiceless sound of fatigue. As she cut her third or fourth goblin throat, she could no longer hide the toll it was taking on her.

Sweat beaded on her forehead. The blade of her stone knife was slick with fat that wouldn't come off no matter how hard she wiped at it.

She looked around, trying to see what her companions were doing. The lizardman carried a sword made from the polished fang of some beast. The white blade had already turned red, but the cutting edge didn't seem to have dulled. It truly must have been forged by some miraculous power.

Goblin Slayer, of course, moved easily from one throat to the next.

And he doesn't even have a special weapon. High Elf Archer watched his hands with the perspicuity of vision only an elvish hunter possessed. As he killed another goblin, he sliced a few fingers off to free the dagger from its hand, and traded his dulled blade for this new one.

I see. The elf slid her own blade back into its sheath and copied him.

She set about killing more of the sleeping monsters. Each one died without knowing that he wasn't the first and wouldn't be the last.

And in the midst of the slaughter, the elf found her anger ebbing.

It was not that she had forgotten the awful sight of the other elf. That was impossible. And yet...

"........."

In her heart, there was a mechanical coldness, strange and new.

She swallowed unconsciously. Her eyes began to wander...in the direction of the man, in his cheap leather armor and steel helm, who was still nonchalantly cutting goblin throats. As he did his work, he took an extra moment to stab each body twice, to ensure it was dead.

How can he think of going it alone? ...Well, I guess he always worked alone before.

What was she to make of this man? The elf didn't know, but even as she was asking this question, her hands were prying the knife from a goblin's fingers.

They finished killing every goblin in the vast hall in a bit less than thirty minutes.

The fine white stone, the captivating drawings on the walls—everything was drenched in goblin gore.

When they call the battlefield a sea of blood, they aren't kidding, the elf thought.

At length, the dwarf and Priestess came breathlessly down from the gallery. Goblin Slayer looked at the gathered adventurers, then pointed deeper inside with his sword. He was covered from head to toe in blood, but…to the elf, it made little difference. The map made it clear there was another room farther in. They would search for any survivors and kill them.

Her eyes met his—at least, she thought they did, though she couldn't see past his helmet. With a nod, Goblin Slayer set off at his bold stride. As ever, he didn't look back.

The world was quiet. What would he do if no one noticed him leaving?

Good grief.

The party looked at one another and smiled noiselessly.

It was Priestess who trailed after him first. The elf followed, her short bow as heavy as a lead weight in her hands. And finally the lizardman and the dwarf joined them, the whole party ready to make their way out of the hall—and that was when it happened.

There was a thump of air. In the silence, it was almost enough to knock them off their feet.

Everyone stood stock-still, staring in the direction they had meant to venture.

Goblin Slayer quickly raised his shield and unsheathed his sword—one of the blades he had taken from a goblin—his attention never wavering.

There was another thump, closer than the first. Something was coming.

Then, out of the darkness, it emerged.

©Noboru Kannatuki

It had a great blue-black body. Horns grew from its forehead, and a putrid stench assaulted them with the creature's every breath. In its hands was a massive war hammer.

The elf's eyes went wide with shock, her voice a strained whisper. "Ogre...!"

The first thing they heard as sound was restored to the world was the echo of that word.

CHAPTER 9

THE STRONG ONES

"I *thought* the goblins were too quiet. Good help is so hard to find these days…" The ogre's mouth was like a rent in his face; his breath heaved out. His voice was a howl. "You aren't like that forest dweller from earlier. You came here knowing this was our fortress, seeking to do us violence." The ogre's bloodlust was palpable, mesmerizing the adventurers. Golden eyes burned in his head.

The party members each readied their weapons, dropping into low stances and preparing for a fight. From their ranks, Goblin Slayer said calmly, "What? You're not a goblin?"

"I am an ogre! Don't tell me you didn't know?!" he bellowed. High Elf Archer took advantage of this exchange to nock an arrow into her short bow.

An ogre. A man-eater.

If goblins were driven by a hatred for those who have words, ogres were moved only by their thirst to hunt prey. These faithless, Unpraying creatures struck fear into the hearts of adventurers everywhere. Anyone who had met an ogre and lived to tell the tale spoke of their fearsomeness and strength.

They said a knight with a sturdy shield died when she tried to block an ogre's attack, only to find her own shield buried in her head.

They said a great warrior had challenged an ogre to a hundred-day battle, but that the monster never took a scratch, and after months of combat, Warrior fell exhausted.

They said a wizard who knew a great many spells had tried to match wits with an ogre but was burned to death when it turned out the ogre knew even more spells than she did.

Suffice it to say, ogres were stiff opponents even for those of Silver rank. A Porcelain rank, they might just squish like a bug.

Fear was written on all the party members' faces. Priestess's trembling arms caused her sounding staff to rattle in her hands.

But Goblin Slayer said with profound exasperation, "No. I didn't know."

There was a tremendous cracking sound—the ogre was grinding his teeth. He looked at the warrior before him, in cheap leather armor and a steel helmet, as though he couldn't believe what he was seeing.

"You cur! You dare to mock me?! I was granted an army by the Demon Generals—"

"Hmm...I knew there had to be someone in charge," Goblin Slayer said, shaking his head. "But I don't know anything about ogres, or Demon Generals, or whatever."

In an excess of fury, the ogre let out a string of unintelligible howls. With every roar, he pounded his war hammer against the walls, shaking the ruins and causing the white stone to crack.

"Then let me teach you about us, ignorant one!" The monster thrust out his great, pallid left hand and began to recite: "*Carbunculus... Crescunt...*" A faint light appeared in his palm and spun until it had become a flame. The flame burned red, then gradually white, and finally blue...

"He's summoning a Fireball!"

"*...Iacta!*"

Dwarf Shaman shouted his warning just as the ogre finished his spell. A sphere of lethally hot fire came flying through the air, trailing a tail like a comet.

"Scatter!" High Elf Archer yelped. The obvious thing to do in the face of an area-of-effect spell like this one was to split up so the entire party wasn't wiped out in one hit. As the party members ran in every direction, one among their number went bounding straight forward.

"O Earth Mother, abounding in mercy, by the power of the land grant safety to we who are weak…"

Priestess stood there, tiny against the great ball of flame, her staff outstretched and her voice raised.

And the Earth Mother, in her mercy, heard her heartfelt supplication. She granted the miracle of Protection.

The fireball came up against an invisible wall and hung in the air, roaring as it burned.

"Hrk…!!" Pressure and heat assailed Priestess, scorching her skin and hands and searing her flesh. Her staff clattered. Sweat beaded on her forehead.

"O…O Earth…*O Earth Mother, abounding in mercy, by the power of the land grant safety to we who are weak!*" Her lips dry, her lungs burning, Priestess repeated the prayer. But the tremendous heat was gradually melting away the invisible barrier…

"Ahhh!" Protection was finally overcome by Fireball. The heat had been somewhat lessened by the spell's long battle with Priestess's miracle, but still, a powerful, hot wind whipped through the atrium, assaulting the adventurers. Moisture evaporated from the air in an instant, and the blood of all the goblin corpses boiled.

But it wasn't enough to cause damage.

"Haa…ahh…" Priestess was on her knees, her tongue hanging out as she gulped air.

She was in a state of Overcast—she had said more prayers than she could handle. The ritual connected her directly to heaven but effaced her own soul, and now her face was pale, and she was impossibly cold.

"I-I-I'm so-so-sorry…!"

"No," Goblin Slayer said, taking a step forward and readying his shield. "You saved us."

Priestess, bent double, nodded vigorously and clung to her staff. "Good work," High Elf Archer said, holding her up. "You'll be all right. Now leave the rest to us."

"Detestable little girl!" the ogre said. "Don't think I will let you have as pleasant an end as that elf!"

"Think you can handle us? Then come and get her!" High Elf

Archer swept in front of Priestess and loosed the arrow from her still-drawn bow.

The ogre swung his hammer and gave a resounding war cry.

"Summon a Dragontooth Warrior," Goblin Slayer said, his attention never lapsing as he held his shield up for protection. "We need more allies." The steel helm did not look away from the ogre, and the sword, an inconveniently short thing he'd taken from a goblin, pointed toward the enemy.

"Well said, milord Goblin Slayer." Lizard Priest made his strange hands-together gesture, then scattered some small fangs on the ground. "*O horns and claws of our father, Iguanodon, thy four limbs, become two legs to walk upon the earth!*" In an instant, the teeth had risen up into a skeletal warrior.

Lizard Priest immediately followed this with the Swordclaw prayer: "*O sickle wings of Velociraptor, rip and tear, fly and hunt!*" The fang he held in his joined hands grew and sharpened before their eyes, until it was the size of a scimitar. The lizardman tossed the newly made weapon to the summoned warrior and drew his own short sword from its sheath.

"The Dragontooth Warrior and I shall go forth with milord Goblin Slayer! Support us from behind!"

"Sure as stone!" The dwarf's reply was as steady as a hammer striking home. He took a handful of dust from his pocket and tossed it into the air.

"*Come out, you gnomes, it's time to work, now don't you dare your duty shirk—a bit of dust may cause no shock, but a thousand make a lovely rock!*"

"Think I'll let you get away with that, you tiny troublemaker?" The ogre ran forward, swinging his hammer. Maybe he meant to burst right through the front line to reach the defender in the rear. He had the power for it.

But he was prevented by the archer, who fired arrow after bud-tipped arrow at him. "Dwarves can learn spells but not how to move their stubby legs, huh?"

"Urraaaghh!" Every arrow found its mark, and one of those marks was the ogre's right eye. He stopped in confusion and retreated, holding his face.

"Pardon me, your long-legged majesty! We've all got to fight as the gods made us!"

In that moment, the dust that had been floating in the air turned into a mass of little rocks that flew at the ogre's huge body. This was the spell Stone Blast.

"Hrrgh! Did you think a parlor trick like that would stop me?" The ogre staggered slightly under the repeated impacts. But no more. The man-eater swept the stones away with his hand and resumed his advance on the adventurers.

Goblin Slayer opposed him alone.

As he danced out, shield on his arm, he made a quick swipe at the monster's legs with his sword.

His movement was small, quick, precise, and as ruthless as ever—

"Hrk...!"

—and it bounced off the ogre with a metallic sound. The monster's skin, even on his legs, was as hard as stone.

"Such impertinence!"

"Hah...?!"

The war hammer swept up and struck the reeling warrior. His armor crumpled, and Goblin Slayer flew through the air, landing in a heap on the ground.

"Orcbolg!!"

"Goblin Slayer, sir!" Priestess and the elf both called out, their faces equally pale.

"I am no mere goblin!" the ogre yelled, ripping the arrow out of his eye and throwing it away. The eye should have been ruined, but instead it bubbled and healed itself and soon shone with malice once more.

So ogres weren't just immensely strong but capable of healing themselves. The elf's teeth began to chatter.

"You stopped my spell. You destroyed my eye. I will take my price for these humiliations!" He raised his hammer again, aiming for Goblin Slayer. "First, I'll tear off your limbs. Then I'll have my sport with your elf and your little Priestess while you watch!"

"Were it so easy, man-eater!" Goblin Slayer's salvation came in the form of the Dragontooth Warrior the lizardman had summoned. The skeletal servant dragged Goblin Slayer away from the blow in the nick of time.

"Goblin Slayer, sir...!!" With wobbling steps, Priestess made her way where the warrior had been evacuated.

"Take care of him, milady Priestess!" The lizardman and the others moved to intercept the advancing ogre.

"Out of my way, you slithering swamp dweller!" The monster brought his hammer down, but the lizardman neatly swept it aside with his tail.

"Master dwarf, milady Ranger—your help, please!"

"Cast a spell, dwarf!"

"I'm on it!"

Running across the shattered floor, the elf fired her arrows in a flood. One branch and then another flew through the air, piercing the ogre's pale flesh.

"You are as irritating as a fly, girl!"

"Wha—? Huh?!"

But that was all they did. The ogre showed no sign of injury, slamming his war hammer into a wall. The elf lost her footing on the quaking floor and was thrown into the air.

A creature without wings is immobile in the air, and this ogre was not one to miss such a chance. He stepped in with a swing of his weapon.

"Whaaat?!"

But neither was the elf one to miss an opportunity. She had curled her body like an acrobat's and slipped past the oncoming hammer.

The ogre's move, however, wasn't meant only to take out the elf. As if to fulfill the monster's vow of vengeance, the ceiling rained rubble from the impact.

"Hrgh!"

"Whoa!"

The lizardman crawled out of the way, and the dwarf rolled to avoid the debris. But the fleshless Dragontooth Warrior was unable to move quickly enough to escape. The stone rained down on it, followed closely by the war hammer. The Dragontooth Warrior shattered, no more than what he had been before, a pile of bones.

He had certainly served his purpose as an extra target, and yet…

"This will not do!" the lizardman cried.

"Did you think to stop me with bones and branches and rocks?!" the ogre howled, breaking off the arrows that riddled his body with a great sweep of his hammer. The elf scrambled away from the pile of debris the previous blow had brought down, eager to avoid a repeat performance.

"At this rate, we're done for!" she shouted, even as she leaped through the air, readying and then loosing another shaft. She had no other option, although the hits seemed to do no damage—and she had only so many arrows.

"This is the last of my spells, too!" the dwarf said, letting off another Stone Blast. The volley of pebbles caused the ogre to flinch but otherwise left him unharmed.

"Is that the best you can do, faeries?!"

"Hrmph, I knew I should've learned Firebolt instead!" The dwarf shook his empty hand with a frown and a cluck. "Or maybe I should've stuck with Stupor."

"The time for such worries is past," the lizardman said lightly, his eyes rolling. "Shall we flee?"

"Wouldn't think of it," the dwarf said merrily. "My grandpappy'd tear out my beard!"

"Agreed. A naga does not run."

As they bantered, the indefatigable Lizard Priest readied his short sword, and the dwarf drew out a sling.

"Ha-ha-ha-ha-haaa! Run out of tricks, adventurers?" The room shook with yet another slam of the monster's hammer. The blow crushed several goblin corpses, sending bits flying into the air. A fragment of goblin landed next to Goblin Slayer, spattering him. He groaned and shifted.

"Goblin Slayer, sir…!" Priestess called to him with tears in her eyes, supporting his head with her hands. With her help, he raised his head at last.

"I can't…quite see… What is happen…ing…?"

"Everyone is still fighting…!"

"I see… Give me a Healing potion. A Stamina potion, too," Goblin

Slayer said calmly, inspecting their supplies at a glance. He sat up stiffly.

Part of his shield and the leather armor over his chest were crushed. His head felt funny somehow, and when he reached up to touch it, he realized there was a dent in his helmet. His whole body ached; every time he drew a breath, pain pierced him...

But pain was a sign he was still alive. Fine.

He had certainly sustained not-insubstantial injuries. But this cheap armor had saved his life.

"Right!"

"Thanks."

Priestess found the bottles in their bags, popped the stoppers, and held them out to him. Goblin Slayer took them stoically and drank down one, then the other. He tossed the bottles aside; they left new scores on the blackened stone floor as they shattered.

Unlike a miracle of the gods, potions like these had relatively minor effects. Goblin Slayer's pain eased a little, but his body still felt like it was made of lead. But he could move. Fine.

"Here we go." Goblin Slayer supported himself with his broken sword as he stood. "Where...is my bag?"

"Um, here it is..."

Her exhausted limbs shook as badly as his hands. But she did not let on or complain. She only pulled the gear close.

"...All right."

Goblin Slayer tore through the contents of his bag, finally coming up with the scroll.

Priestess paled. She looked at Goblin Slayer; to her eyes, he was blurred by tears. "You can't..."

"If it will win this fight, I certainly can." He shook his head gently. "And if this works...things won't be so bad, anyway." He pushed her hand away and stood, then stepped forth.

He heard dripping as blood from some wound stained the floor red under his feet. So long as it didn't cause him to slip, he didn't care.

"Orcbolg!" High Elf Archer shouted as she saw him.

"I have a plan. Here goes."

"Sure thing! Do it!" High Elf Archer didn't ask what the plan was, only loosed another arrow from her bow.

"Right, Beard-cutter! I've faith in you!"

"Regrettably, we are most hard put here."

Dwarf Shaman and Lizard Priest nodded to each other, then leaped out of the fray under the cover of the elf's arrows.

But...

"Oh...!" High Elf Archer bit her lip.

Goblin Slayer stepped out in front of them, raised his broken shield, and took a deep stance. His wounds were obviously severe. One more hit could sunder his flesh and bones, could kill him.

No, wait... High Elf Archer shook her head. *He's looking for his chance...* He would do something. If there was anything to be done, he would find it. *So let me do my part, too...*

The dwarf grabbed rubble from the ground and fired them from his sling. The lizardman dashed toward the ogre, slashing with his claws. And of course, the elf's arrows fell like rain.

"You insects! You aggravating little bugs!"

The ogre, arrows lodged all over his body, was infuriated. His war hammer flew this way and that with a sound like a storm. Every blow brought down more rubble and caused the corpses to dance on the ground.

Through it all, Goblin Slayer kept his distance, never flinching.

The ogre looked down with disgust at the half-dead warrior, and then, twisting his face hideously, he laughed.

"Come to think of it, as I recall, your tiny friend was all out of miracles...out of strength..." He thrust out his giant palm. "*Carbunculus... Crescunt...*" The familiar white ball of flame began forming in his palm as he intoned the words.

Someone gulped.

"Ah... Oh!" Priestess tried to stand but tumbled back to the ground. Her sounding staff fell from her shaking hands.

"Don't worry. If perchance she survives this, I promise not to kill her...right away."

The fire in the ogre's hand shone white, then finally blue, threatening to scorch the adventurers. There was no way to stop it.

"I have food, after all. What I need is someone to help me rebuild the ranks of my goblins."

At that moment, Goblin Slayer leaped true as an arrow at the expanding ball of flame.

The ogre snorted. What could this warrior do to him? This dying adventurer?

"Let me grant your wish, boy! I will burn you until not even ashes remain!" The last of the words of power, the words that could alter the very way of the world, spilled out of him and into the roiling flame.

"Iacta!"

The fireball flew from the ogre's palm. It seemed to set the very air aflame.

Death raced toward them.

Priestess—or was it High Elf Archer?—screamed.

Lizard Priest and Dwarf Shaman moved to protect the women.

And then:

"Fool."

The lone, calm word of a man meeting his foe.

A roar.

A flash.

And finally, silence.

"Hmm... Hrr?" The ogre could not understand what had happened.

He felt himself floating. And then his massive body was slammed into a pile of rubble.

Perhaps he had made the fireball too powerful and been a bit stunned by the kickback. Or was this a ploy of his little opponents?

In fact, it was neither.

"Hrgh...?!" The ogre lost his breath with the impact. He could see his own legs.

Only they weren't attached to him anymore.

Goblin Slayer walked toward the ogre, smoke rising from him. It finally dawned on the ogre that he had been cut in half.

"Grr... Hrrrghh!" When he opened his mouth to speak, he immediately began to retch blood. At the same moment, his nose filled with the smell of iron and another odd scent.

Salt.

The chamber was flooding with seawater.

The water was red with blood: the ogre's, Goblin Slayer's.

Why?! What happened?! What…what did you do to me?!

As the ogre writhed in pain, his insides spilling into the open air, a cool voice answered him:

"The scroll contained the spell Gate."

Goblin Slayer undid the knot and revealed the magical scroll being burned away by a supernatural flame. The fire continued to lick at the page even as it was inundated with water until finally the scroll vanished without a trace.

"It opens onto the bottom of the sea." As Goblin Slayer spoke, the elf—indeed, everyone—was lost for words.

Scrolls fetch a good price, but every once in a great while, there is an adventurer who does not wish to part with one.

An ancient artifact, this scroll had contained the lost spell Gate. Write the destination on it with the words of power, and it would open a door to that place. For an adventurer, it could be a powerful weapon or a life-saving escape route. But the chances of such an item showing up in a marketplace were next to nil. If you wanted one, you had to scour deep dungeons and ancient ruins for yourself…

…and even then, you needed a Platinum tag or a lot of luck to find one. Goblin Slayer had used his scroll without hesitation—and then not even to escape, but to attack. After he had paid Witch at the Adventurers Guild a pretty penny to connect the scroll to the bottom of the sea.

The pent-up seawater had come flying out with such force that it instantly extinguished the fireball and cut the ogre in two.

"Hrg! Yarr! Graaaa!!"

The ogre dumbly watched his legs fall to the floor. He flailed in the pool of water, sputtering and coughing blood. He showed no sign of healing himself. Ogres have great powers of regeneration, but even they can't pull themselves back from the brink of death.

I'm going to…die? Me? Die?!

"Grrrrawwwwwoooooohhhh!!"

Perhaps it was the lack of blood to his brain, but the ogre was seized with an inarticulate terror. He gave a great, pathetic wail.

He couldn't understand it.

"Now...what did you say you were?" The man strode toward the ogre and stood above him.

Not a goblin, was it?

The words rolled around the ogre's head like an echo.

That meant... That meant...

He had prepared that spell...just to kill some goblins!

"Never mind. It doesn't matter."

The ogre made to speak—whether to beg for his life or to taunt them one last time, he himself didn't know. But his last words never made it out of his mouth. Goblin Slayer crushed the ogre's throat under his heel. The ogre gave a final voiceless gasp, looking vacantly up at the pitiless steel helmet.

"You are nowhere near as frightening..."

The man raised his sword. This was it. The end. The ogre saw cold eyes shining from the darkness inside that helm.

"...as the goblins I've faced."

The ogre's consciousness was consumed with pain and humiliation, fear and despair; then it was submerged in darkness; then it was extinguished.

§

When they emerged from the ruins, they found an elven carriage waiting for them. The Dragontooth Warrior had successfully escorted the prisoner home, and her people had hurriedly sent a party to the ruins. The warriors who accompanied the carriage carried, to an elf, pristine gear. All of it made only from the bounty of the earth: wood and leather and stone.

"Well met! What lies in these ruins? Are the goblins—?"

But the adventurers climbed straight into the carriage. Even the dwarf, who might normally have had some choice words for elves, said nothing.

They were all completely drained.

"...At any rate, we shall search within," one of the warriors said gruffly. "Please have a pleasant ride to town." And with that, they disappeared into the ruins.

The coachman gave a shout to the horses, and the carriage began rolling with a clatter of hooves.

The sun set without the party even noticing, and the moons ran their course. Soon the sun was rising again. The light of dawn shone in the pale sky from across the horizon. It must have taken all night to reach town.

The traveling companions left their weapons wrapped in coverings. Each was at their ease; no one moved. Well, almost no one.

High Elf Archer shifted until her mouth was near Priestess's ear.

"Hey...," she said.

"Yes...?" Priestess looked up idly. She was bone-tired, spent from her soul-effacing prayers, and yet she wore a brave smile.

"Is he always like that? I mean, does he always pull that sort of stunt?" The elf looked no better than Priestess, black and red with gore and barely able to keep her eyes open. She indicated Goblin Slayer, slumped against a wooden box.

He still wore his dented armor and held his cracked sword...but he was finally asleep. Every trace of his wounds had been wiped away by Lizard Priest's Refresh spell. It was no surprise that it was so much more powerful than Priestess's Minor Heal. That was simply the difference between a Porcelain and a Silver rank.

The problem..., he mused, swishing his tail, *the problem is accumulated fatigue.*

After finishing off the ogre, Goblin Slayer had wanted to make a sweep for any surviving goblins. Even though it had been clear he was the most exhausted member of a drained party. And he was trying so hard not to show it...

"Yes...," Priestess said with a strained expression. "He's always like this."

"Hmm..."

"But you'd be...surprised how much he cares for those around him." She touched his armor with her slender finger. He didn't stir. She stroked the dirty leather gently. "He doesn't have to help us. Or teach us. But he does."

"Hmm," the elf murmured again.

She was angry.

She couldn't reconcile herself to what had happened. That was no adventure. How could anyone call it that?

"I can't help it. I can't stand Orcbolg."

And that was that.

I thought adventures were supposed to be fun.

This was no adventure.

It didn't have the excitement or gratification of discovering new things, the joy of experiencing the unknown.

She was left with only an empty weariness.

So there were people out there who did nothing but hunt goblins, never finding a single pleasure in their "adventures."

To her, it was unforgivable.

She was an adventurer. She had left the forest because she loved adventure.

The elf nodded with conviction. Yes. Someday she would show him. Maybe not right away, perhaps, but someday.

"I'll show him what a real adventure is."

For if she didn't, he—and all of them—might be lost...

Heyo! I slew some goblins! I've come to make my report.

Huh? Why're you so surprised? I know I'm alone. Can't one person normally handle some goblins?

Hmm…? Who's that? They look real important.

A sorcerer from the Capital? But they're so short!

Whoa, sorry, sorry! Don't get angry. I just thought it was cool.

My report? Oh yeah. Um… Let's see. I guess I'll start at the beginning.

I was brought up at the Temple, but I turned fifteen, so I had to leave. I decided to become an adventurer…

And there was this quest to slay some goblins in an old cave near this village. I mean, everyone starts with goblins, right?

Anyway, it was less of a cave than some ancient ruins. They looked just like in all the stories. Inside, it looked…it kind of looked like the Temple in town.

Huh? Goblins? Oh yeah, there were some. A lot, actually. They kept coming at me, so I kept cutting them down. I got blood all over me, and they stink. It was a real pain.

Poison? That's what antidotes are for, right? A helmet? Those things get so hot. Plus, my hair is too long for them.

And then, um… Where was I? Oh, right. I was saying how it looked like the Temple inside. As far in as you could go, there was this pedestal, and when I went up to it, I met this big old boss. He was all, "I am one of the sixteen Generals of Hell!" or whatever. He was really full of himself. Even though he was just some goblin. He was a goblin, wasn't he?

I guess there are some strong goblins, though. He was actually using spells on me! But I've got some spells, too. I used Firebolt. Maybe…five or six times? I wasn't counting. That made me pretty tired, so I was like, "Time to end this!" but when I tried to stab him, my sword broke!

Then he comes at me! "I'm going to eat your liver!" he says. I hate to admit it, but…well, let's say I was wearing clean underwear when I went in there.

A-anyhow, I was pretty worried because I didn't have a sword, but I reached right out for the pedestal. Why? Well, because there was a sword buried in it. Like the one in the symbol of the Supreme God. I didn't care if it was old; I just needed a weapon. The sword popped right out, and guess what? It was still shiny, like it was brand-new!

It didn't take much after that. The boss made a nasty scream when I cut him in half. "You may kill me," he says, "but the other fifteen will hunt you! You'll have no rest, to the ends of the earth they'll pursue you!" I mean, what*ever*, right? Fifteen goblins, fifty goblins, who cares?

What do you mean, do I plan to fight them?

…Huh? The ancient spirits of evil have returned? The guy I killed was one of their generals? And this is the sword of light?

Pfft. As if. I can't be the legendary hero, can I?

I mean, I'm a girl!

CHAPTER 10

DOZING

Even now, he remembered one time when his older sister had scolded him roundly.

It was when he had made that girl, his old friend, cry.

Why? Right... Because she was taking a trip to the city. She was going to stay at a farm.

She'd been telling him all about it. He'd grown jealous. He couldn't help himself.

He didn't know anything about life outside their village. He didn't know the name of the mountains in the distance or anything that lay beyond them.

He knew that if you followed the road long enough, you would come to a city, but what that meant, what kind of city it was, he didn't know.

At a younger age, he'd thought he would become an adventurer. He would leave the village, maybe slay a dragon or two, and then come home as a hero—a Platinum-ranked adventurer.

Of course, after he'd seen a few more birthdays come and go, he had realized that was impossible.

No—not impossible.

But he would have to leave his sister. The sister who had raised him after their mother and father died.

He *could* have become an adventurer. But he decided not to choose that path.

That was why he'd been angry at his friend.

As his sister led him home by the hand, she scolded him.

"When you get angry at someone, you become a goblin!" and "You're supposed to protect girls!"

His sister was wise.

It wasn't that she had a great deal of knowledge, but her mind was sharp. Maybe the sharpest in the village. In fact, she earned her food by teaching the local children to read and write. Children were needed to work on their families' farms, but literacy was important, too.

In all things, she tried to impart to her little brother the importance of using his head. If you just keep thinking, she told him, you'll come up with something eventually.

His sister must have dreamed of going to the city to study. But she stayed in the village for his sake. So he would stay, too. For hers.

To him, it was the obvious thing.

When they got home, his sister made him a stew of milk and chicken meat. He loved his sister's stew. He would ask for another bowl, and then another, but now he couldn't remember how it had tasted.

No doubt because that was the last time he'd had it before *they* came...

§

He opened his eyes slowly.

He raised himself off the reed mat and looked up at a familiar ceiling.

His body still ached. He gradually stretched his limbs, then calmly took his clothes in hand. An unadorned hempen shirt. It was faded from repeated washings and smelled faintly of soap. The shirt kept him from burning in the sun. And it covered the scars that were all over his body.

He pulled on the ordinary hempen shirt, then cotton gambeson.

He went to put on his steel helmet and armor, then remembered he had given them to a shop to repair.

He had no shield, either. It had taken a critical hit from that ogre.

"...Hmph."

There was nothing to be done about it. He put his sword at his hip for a bare minimum of security. His field of view seemed exceptionally wide and bright, his head too light, and it unsettled him.

"Good morning! You sure slept well!" The voice came at him like a surprise attack.

It was that girl, his old friend, leaning into his room, her chest resting on the sill of the open window.

A breeze blew into the room. He hadn't felt the air of early summer on his bare skin like this in a long time.

His friend was in her work clothes. A little sweat beaded on her forehead. From the light that poured in, he guessed the sun was already high in the sky.

"Sorry," he said, offering the laconic word in apology for oversleeping. It looked like she had already started in on caring for the animals. He had completely missed the chance to help.

She waved it away, no hint of annoyance in her tone. "Oh, no, it's fine. You need rest more than anything. I know you do, because otherwise, you would never miss your morning inspection. Did you sleep well?"

"Yes."

"It looks like it'll be a hot one today. Sure you won't be too warm in those clothes?"

"...Maybe you're right," he said with a slow nod. She was right. And really, the bulky cotton would get in the way while he was working. So he tore off the underarmor he had put on just moments before and tossed it on the bed.

"Gosh, you don't have to be so rough with it. You'll tear it."

"I don't care."

"Of course you don't..." She gave a deep shrug and narrowed her eyes like she was babysitting some young boy. "Well, fine by me. I'm hungry. Uncle should be up by now. Let's hurry and have breakfast."

"Fine," he answered calmly and left his room. He strode down the hallway.

The master of the house, already seated at the table in the dining area, went wide-eyed when he saw the figure in the doorway.

"Good morning, sir."

"Ye...yeah. Morning."

He paid Uncle's reaction no mind, but only gave a courteous nod and sat down across from him. Uncle shifted uncomfortably.

"You've, uhh, you're up rather late today…"

"Yes." He nodded firmly. "I overslept. I will do my inspection later."

"I see…" The acknowledgment came out almost as a groan. He opened his mouth, then closed it again, then furrowed his eyebrows. "You ought to…rest for a while. Can't work if you don't have your strength, right?"

He was silent for a moment, then nodded. "True."

This was as close as they came to a conversation.

He knew the owner of the farm was a good person. He treated the girl, his niece, like his own daughter. But he also knew the owner did not like him, or at least found him discomfiting.

It was each person's choice whom they liked and disliked. *He* certainly didn't need to try to convince Uncle one way or the other.

"Whew! Sorry it took so long! I'll put out the food in a second, so dig in!" His old friend came running in moments later and began to set out dishes on the table. Cheese and bread and a creamy soup. All made fresh on the farm. He ate greedily, as always. When he had finished, he piled the empty plates, pushed his chair back noisily, and stood.

"I'm going."

"What? Aw, shoot, time to make the deliveries already?" At his words, she began to clean up hurriedly. She stuffed a piece of bread into her mouth in a rather unbecoming way. Watching her, the owner of the farm pinched up his mouth reluctantly.

"The cart again?"

"Oh, Uncle, you're such a worrywart. I keep telling you, I'm a lot stronger than I look…"

"I'll take them," he said shortly. The girl and her uncle exchanged a look. Had he not been clear enough?

"I will take them," he repeated. She seemed confused, not quite looking at him, then she shook her head.

"No, you…you don't have to do that. You need to rest."

"My body will go soft," he said calmly. "Besides, I have business at the Guild." He knew he didn't say much. He couldn't remember if he had always been that way. But he knew that however brief he might be, she was always looking for ways to take care of him.

All the more reason he should say clearly what he had to say.

"It's all right," he said, and he left the dining area.

He could hear her quick footsteps as she hurried after him.

The cart was waiting just outside. The deliveries for the Adventurers Guild had been loaded up the night before. He tugged on the ropes to make sure everything was secure, then picked up the crossbar and began to push.

The wheels creaked to life, rumbling along the gravel path. He could feel the weight in his arms.

"Are you sure you're all right?" Just as he reached the gate, she came running up, breathing hard. She peered at his face.

"Yes." He nodded shortly, then gave another push.

The tree-lined road ran all the way to the city. He went slowly, one step after the next, feeling the earth under his feet.

Just as she'd said, the day seemed likely to get hot. It was not yet noon, and already the sun's rays were pounding down. He was perspiring within moments. He should've brought a hand towel.

He was just figuring that if it didn't get in his eyes no harm was done when something soft brushed his forehead.

"What happened to getting some rest?" Her cheeks puffed out in annoyance as she dabbed at his forehead with her own handkerchief. "You collapsed the minute you got back and slept for days. Do you know how worried I was?" He pretended to think for a moment, then shook his head. Surely it wasn't that important.

"That was already three days ago."

"It was *only* three days ago! That's why I said not to overdo it," she said as she reached out and wiped his face. "You could barely stand up! You need to rest."

Still pulling the cart, he sighed. "You…"

"Huh?"

"…are a lot like your uncle."

She looked like she couldn't quite decide whether that made her happy or angry. Either way, she didn't seem prepared to back off.

"It's just a little overwork. You don't have to worry about me," he explained with a hint of annoyance.

No. It wasn't annoyance. He just hated to be reminded that he could barely look after his own health.

But I need to be reminded. So that I won't make the same mistake twice.

"Is that what your Priestess friend told you?" Her voice had an edge to it. He glanced at her out of the corner of his eye and saw that her cheeks were still puffed a bit in a sulk.

"No."

He gazed forward again and threw himself into another push of the cart.

"Another party member said that."

"Hmm," she said, mollified. "You're adventuring with a lot of new people these days."

"We've only been on one quest."

"It sounds like you're planning to go on more, then?"

He couldn't answer. He didn't know what to say.

It would be a lie to say he had no such intention. There were worse things. But would he go out of his way to invite them on his next quest...?

At that moment, the wind came up. He closed his eyes, hearing the rustling of the branches and basking in the light that filtered through the leaves.

They stopped talking.

The breeze. Their footsteps. Their breath. The rumble of the wheels turning.

A bird sang somewhere. A child shouted at play. The tumult of the city was still far off.

"This is nice." The murmur suddenly came from his lips.

"What...?"

"This is nicer than hunting goblins."

"Gee, you really know how to charm a girl."

"I see..."

Apparently, he was still not communicating clearly.

If you didn't know what to say, it was better not to say anything. From the corner of his eye, he took in her confused expression. He kept pushing the cart in silence.

"Heh-heh!" she laughed suddenly. Almost as if she herself hadn't expected it.

"What?"

"Nothing!"

"Really?"

"Really."

She walked along, humming a tune he didn't recognize. Still, he didn't have to recognize it. She was happy. That was enough.

They parked the cart at the back entrance and came into the lobby of the Guild. All was calm. It was almost noon, so of course most of the adventurers had already set out. Or maybe they were all up at the Capital, which had seen a good deal of trouble lately. He didn't know. In the Guild Hall, there were a few quest givers filing paperwork and a few adventurers he knew cooling their heels, but that was it. Very few people seemed to be sitting around waiting for anyone, and the line to see Guild Girl was short.

"Perfect," his old friend said with a happy clap. "I won't have to wait forever to get the signature I need. I'll take care of that and be right back, but…you said you had something to do, too, didn't you?"

"Yes."

"Okay. Well, when you're done, we can meet up here and go home together!"

"All right."

He watched her run off smiling, then took a look around the lobby.

He didn't see who he was looking for. Maybe he was a little early.

In that case, he would wait in his usual seat by the wall. He headed over with his characteristic bold stride…

"Hrm…?"

…and almost ran smack into a person sitting in the chair. That person looked up at him suspiciously. It was the spear-wielding adventurer.

Spearman slumped in the chair, limbs akimbo, glaring openly at him.

"Never seen anyone so fit but so pale. I don't recognize your face. You new around here?"

"No." He shook his head once as he spoke. Of course, the man recognized him. And of course, he wasn't new.

But it seemed Spearman refused to believe it was really him without his usual armor. Spearman addressed him in the tone one might use with an unfamiliar colleague.

"Guess you wouldn't be. Adventurers who want to make money these days go to the Capital, huh?" he said. "You must be here for a break or something."

The newcomer nodded at "something," and Spearman laughed.

"Capital's a rough place. I can see why you'd want to take a little time off." With a nimble move, he straightened up and adjusted his grip on his spear. "I hear over there everyone's worried about evil spirits or something. A battle to save the world? Sounds like a hell of a way to make a name for yourself."

"Aren't you going there?"

"Me? Don't be ridiculous. The only thing I fight for is me. Not money and not the fate of the world.

"Well," Spearman amended, "me and..." He gave Guild Girl a significant look.

When the newcomer let his gaze drift over to the front desk as well, he saw Guild Girl running around behind it like an excited puppy. Apparently, a crowd of adventurers wasn't the only thing that kept the Guild busy.

"...personal reasons," Spearman finished. "I don't need some motto, some rallying cry."

"Don't you, now?"

"I don't." So saying, Spearman flopped back in the chair.

Both of them saw the sensuous Witch slinking toward them.

"Well, see you," Spearman said. "I've got a date with—or should I say *in*—some ruins. Wish me luck!"

"I will." He nodded quietly.

"You're a real people person," Spearman said with a laugh, and: "That's not all bad."

As the two of them left the room, Witch looked back at this "people person" and gave him a broad, meaningful wink and a laugh.

"Take care, now," she said.

"I will."

And then he sat down in the newly empty chair.

He stared vacantly up at the high ceiling of the Guild Hall. It was only now dawning on him that Spearman and Witch were in a party together. And here he'd thought he knew both of them rather well.

"Um, Goblin Slayer, sir! Goblin Slayer, are you here, sir?!"

This time, a hesitant voice. He shifted his gaze toward the sound but didn't move his head, a habit from wearing his helmet for so long.

He saw the apprentice boy from the workshop, standing there in a conspicuously grease-stained leather apron.

"That's me."

"Oh, thank goodness. I didn't know who you were. The boss is asking for you. He says the work's done."

"All right. I'll be right there."

The Adventurers Guild wasn't just for handing out quests; it hosted all kinds of entrepreneurial activity. Besides the offices, there was an inn, a tavern, an item shop, and an equipment shop. Of course, it wasn't absolutely necessary to have stores like these be a part of the Guild building, not really. But as far as the state was concerned, it was convenient to keep the ruffians in one place as much as possible rather than have them wandering the city.

When he stood up and walked off, it was to one of the workshops at the Guild. Through the building, into another room farther in. In front of a glowing forge stood an old man relentlessly swinging a hammer, working a sword that had just come out of the mold into a true, tempered weapon.

Granted, it was a mass-production item that didn't take too much to forge; nothing compared to the swords of legend. But then, too, the ability to forge essentially the same sword, over and over, with almost no variation, was a remarkable talent.

"...You're here." The old man eyed him. The blacksmith's facial hair was so full he could have passed for a dwarf. It might have been long hours at the forge that caused him to squint one eye nearly shut and open the other unnaturally wide. It was not an attractive look.

"You place order after order but only for the cheapest goods. Tell me, how'm I supposed to fill my coffers that way?"

"Sorry."

"Don't be sorry. Just be more careful with my products."

"I'll try."

"Hrmph," the old man muttered, "wouldn't know a joke if it bit him in the… Hmph. Over here." He beckoned. When Goblin Slayer approached, the smith thrust the armor and helmet at him.

"Should be fine, but try 'em on to be sure. I'll adjust them if need be. No charge."

"Thank you."

His dirty, bent, crushed armor had been made good as— Well, not as good as new, but as good as it had been before his encounter with the ogre. At the very least, he could trust it with his life once more.

"And a scroll? Were you able to get one?"

"You gave me the gold, so I'll get you the goods. But scrolls are rare. And expensive." The old man gave an angry snort and turned back to the forge. He pulled out the simple iron sword he had crafted, inspected it, then returned it to the fire with a cluck of his tongue. "When some adventurer finds one and comes to sell it, I'll get it for you, but that's as much as I can do."

"I know. That's enough." He passed a bag of gold coins to the apprentice, then walked to a corner of the workshop where he would be out of the way.

The smith had even attached a new cotton-padded gambeson to wear for protection under his armor. How kind of him.

Gloves, mail coat, armor, chest plate, and then the helmet. He put on the equipment mechanically, in his accustomed order. As he did so, he heard the puzzled voice of the apprentice boy.

"Hey, boss. That guy's a Silver-ranked adventurer, right?"

"So I hear."

"Why's he use that armor? If he wanted to move silently, we have mithril mail or…"

"Don't you know, boy?"

"No, sir. Why not a good magical sword instead of a scroll or…"

"Because only a munchkin would be dumb enough to take some enchanted blade to deal with goblins!" The smith struck the iron with all his strength, a clear sound ringing out as the hammer met the sword.

"That is a man who knows his business."

§

Aren't I popular today? he thought. As he came back from the workshop to the lobby, he saw someone rushing toward him. *Tap-tap-tap* footfalls were accompanied by the bouncing of a gorgeous chest and a face wreathed in a smile.

"Goblin Slayer, sir!" Priestess waved as she bounded over to him.

"Yes, what?"

"Here, look at this!"

She reached breathlessly into her sleeve and pulled out her rank tag. It was no longer porcelain white but a gleaming obsidian.

Oh. Is that what this is about?

He nodded to his beaming companion. "You've moved up from tenth rank to ninth."

"Yes, sir! I've been promoted!" The rank system adventurers lived by was based on the amount of good an adventurer had done in the world—some referred to this as "experience points" or the like, but it was, in essence, based on the rewards they had earned for hunting. Those who had earned a certain amount could be promoted in rank, pending a brief personal evaluation. There could hardly have been an issue with Priestess's personality, so this promotion was effectively an acknowledgment of her growing strength. "I wasn't sure they would give it to me, but I think that battle with the ogre counted for a lot…" She scratched one blushing cheek with her finger.

"I see."

What's an ogre again?

Oh, right—it was that creature they'd encountered beneath the ruins, wasn't it? He nodded. So their little expedition had been quite important, in the end. After a moment's thought he added shortly:

"Good for you."

"I owe it all to you, sir!" Her gaze, her beautiful eyes, bored into him. He caught his breath. What should he say? There was a long pause.

"Not at all," he finally squeaked out. "I didn't do anything."

"You did so much!" she responded with a grin. "You saved me when we first met."

"But I couldn't save your companions."

"True, but..." Her face stiffened for a moment. She couldn't quite finish her sentence—understandably.

Even he still remembered the awful scene all too clearly. Warrior, Wizard, Fighter, who had all lost everything. Her party had been trodden into the dust.

Priestess swallowed but continued resolutely. "But you did save me. I want to at least thank you for that." Then she smiled. On her face, the smile was like a fresh bloom. "So, thank you!" she said with a deep bow. Goblin Slayer, predictably, was at a loss for words.

Priestess said she would go to the Temple and let the Mother Superior know about her promotion. He stood, watching her depart with her delicate steps and her hands wrapped tightly around her sounding staff.

He was silent.

He looked over at the front desk, where his old friend still seemed occupied with paperwork.

"I'm going to unload the cart," he said, and she waved in response.

He left the foyer and headed for the entrance of the Guild Hall. He took the vegetables and produce from the cart one by one and set them near the entrance to the kitchen. Working under the hot sun, sweat began to bead on his forehead beneath his helmet in no time.

But it was important to protect the head. He couldn't let down his guard. That's what he was thinking when:

"Hey... You have a moment?" a cool voice called out suddenly from behind him.

He put down his load and turned around slowly.

"Orcbolg? What are you doing...?" It was High Elf Archer. Her long ears were standing straight up.

"What, Beard-cutter is here? So he is! Should you be up and about yet?"

"I heard you slumbered for three days...but you seem perfectly hale now."

"His footsteps give him away, don't they?" the elf replied to the dwarf and the lizardman, who were lined up with her. It seemed the three had settled in the city after their goblin-slaying trip.

Traditionally, adventurers had always been wanderers, changing their base of operations whenever it was convenient or necessary.

"This is a nice place," the elf said, "very comfortable. But what *are* you doing?" She leaned in with great interest.

"I'm unloading this cart."

"Hmm... Wait, don't tell me... You're strapped for cash, so you took a job as a delivery boy."

"No," he said annoyed. "Did you want something?"

"Oh yeah. This guy, uh..." The elf trailed off meaningfully, jerking her thumb at Lizard Priest. The lizardman's tongue flicked up to his nose and back. His hands fidgeted incessantly.

"Milord Goblin Slayer, I... Hrm..."

"What?"

"I humbly request, some...haa..."

"What is it?" Goblin Slayer asked.

Dwarf Shaman interceded with a smirk. "Scaly here wants some cheese."

"He ought to just come out and say it," High Elf Archer suggested, narrowing her eyes like a cat. The lizardman hissed at them, but the two seemed to pay him no mind. Perhaps they were pleased to have seen this side of their otherwise unflappable companion. It was normally the lizardman who was the mediator for the group.

Goblin Slayer could see he wasn't going to get out of this. They had been together for only one quest so far. There were too many things he didn't know.

"Will this do?"

He opened one of the packages on the cart, pulled out a round of cheese, and tossed it to them.

"Oh-ho!" The lizardman caught it, and his eyes rolled wide in his head.

"You can pay the Guild for it."

"Yes, yes, understood, milord Goblin Slayer! Oh, sweet nectar! It is worth its weight in gold!" He was practically dancing. He opened his mouth and took a big bite of cheese.

The elf gave a helpless smile. "I guess even the most serious guys have to let themselves go every once in a while," she said.

"I see." Goblin Slayer nodded. He didn't feel bad about it. He reached for the next item on the cart.

He grabbed hold of the wooden crate, picked it up, set it down. Then the next and the next. It was simple work, but he didn't dislike it. When he looked up from it a few crates later, though, there was the elf, still standing there.

She shifted restlessly as she watched him at the repetitive job.

"Wh-what? Should I not be here?"

"No." He shook his head slightly. "But it's going to be hot today."

"Li...listen!" Her voice was a little too loud. Her ears bobbed up and down, up and down.

"What now?" he asked with a sigh.

"Um, we're...we're checking out some ruins now..."

"Ruins."

"Yeah, like we went to on our last quest. Trying to figure out what the evil spirits are planning and everything..."

"I see."

"But our party doesn't have a good forward guard, right?" *I mean, I'm a ranger; he's a priest. Shorty is a spell caster.* She played with her hair as she spoke and didn't quite look at him.

"Right," he agreed. Everything she'd said was true.

"So, I mean..." She trailed off and looked at the ground. He waited for her to continue. "I thought maybe...maybe we should talk to you..."

He was silent. *Was that it?* He lifted another box without a word.

The elf's ears drooped, and he set the box back down.

"I'll think about it."

He could practically hear her ears spring up. "Right! Sure! You do that!" With a little wave, she set out for the front of the Guild Hall. The dwarf followed her, stroking his beard with one hand and pulling along the lizardman—still entranced by his delicious prize—with the other.

"How about that, Beard-cutter? Life's so hard for long-ears. She ought to just come out and ask you along!"

"Quiet, dwarf. I'm not out of arrows yet."

"I'm quivering in me boots, lass." It seemed the elf was not out of earshot. Goblin Slayer watched the two walk off, bickering loudly.

Before he knew it, he was almost done unloading the cart. He let out a puff of breath and shook his helmet. The sun was high in the sky. It was nearly summer.

Then...

"Yaaah!"

"Heeeeyah!"

Suddenly, shouts rang out, accompanied by the clear tone of metal on metal.

The sound of a sword fight. And it wasn't sudden. He just hadn't been paying attention.

He craned his neck to find the source of the disturbance. It was coming from the plaza behind the Guild building—right in front of him.

"Ha-ha-ha, you call that a strike? You couldn't kill a goblin that way!"

"Damn! He's too big; he's getting in my guard! Circle around right!"

"All right, here we go!"

A heavily armored warrior was wielding a great sword as easily as a matchstick and fending off thrusts from two young boys. One of the boys was the scout from the heavily armored warrior's party, and the other...he was the rookie warrior who had been headed to the sewers. His movements had the broad character of an inexperienced Porcelain rank, but he was doing well in that he was trying to find the flow of combat.

"Not a bad plan," the overdressed warrior responded, "but it doesn't work if you shout it to your opponent!"

"Yrrrahhh?!"

"Waaagh!"

The gulf of experience and strength was simply too great. Warrior handled them easily.

It seemed Goblin Slayer was a bit too conspicuous as he stood watching them train.

"Well, if it isn't Goblin Slayer," said a low voice with more than a hint of suspicion. It was the woman in knight's armor. As he recalled, she was also part of the armored warrior's team.

"Haven't seen you for a few days," he called. "I was starting to think that ogre put an end to you. But here you are, alive and well."

"Yes."

"…Is that how you talk to everyone you know?"

"Yes."

"…I see…" Knight furrowed her brow as if she had a headache and gave a measured shake of her head.

He didn't think it was as strange as all that, but he kept it to himself. He did say, however, "I didn't think that warrior was a member of your party."

"Oh. He's not. We were doing some sparring with the kid here…" Apparently, they had noticed the other young warrior practicing his sword work nearby and invited him to join in.

Most of the would-be warriors who came up from the country with a sword and a dream were self-taught in the use of their weapons. Even this one chance to train with a real adventurer might save the boy's life someday.

"Now I've just got to teach those girls to act like ladies…"

Across from where the scout and the young swordsman were boldly facing down Warrior in his heavy armor, a cleric and druid girl were leaning against a low wall, watching the match with undisguised excitement.

"And that meathead is probably getting tired about now. Maybe I ought to jump in," Knight said, with a twisted bit of a grin. She hefted her huge shield and her sword—her pride and joy—and jumped over the wall and into the fray. "All right, now you're in trouble! I thought I heard there were some mighty warriors here, but all I see are a couple of weaklings!"

"Whaat? How can you even be a paladin talking like that?!"

"Here's my answer!"

"Some training!" groaned Warrior, who always attacked from the front—this was why people liked him. His great sword spun like a hurricane, his huge shield stopping one blow after another. He danced away from each sharp retort and found an opening in return. Cleric and the druid girl were just coming to the aid of the hard-pressed young men when...

"That knight can't quite mind her own business, can she?" A laugh as clear as a bell followed. When had someone come up beside him?

"Pardon the intrusion, my dear Goblin Slayer, but how about you drink this? It's very hot out here..." She had come out the kitchen door. Now she offered him a cup.

"Thanks," he said, taking it. He gulped it down with one great slosh into his helmet. It was cold and sweet.

"It's got a bit of lemon and honey in it," Guild Girl said. "It's supposed to be good for fatigue." He nodded in agreement. It might make a good addition to his field provisions. He would have to remember it.

"There's some talk these days about a new building that would be dedicated to that kind of training," she said, nodding at the sparring party.

"Oh?" He dabbed at the beads of liquid on his lips.

"We could hire some retired adventurers to teach. So many beginners just don't know anything at all." *If we could teach them even a little bit, maybe more of them would come home.* She looked into the distance and smiled. Guild Girl had seen many adventurers come...and go. That it was only the paperwork she had to deal with didn't soften the blow. It wasn't hard to understand why she would want to help newcomers.

"And...," she added. "Even after you retire, you still have to live. Everyone needs something to fill the time."

"Is that right?" He gave the empty cup back to her.

"Yes, it is," she insisted with her usual peppy nod, her braids bouncing. "So you'd better take care of yourself, too, all right?"

He was quiet a moment. "That seems to be everyone's advice for me lately."

"I'm going to wait until you're healed up before I give you any more quests. Maybe a month."

"Erk..." He groaned.

"And next time you work till you collapse, six months."

"That would...be a problem."

"Wouldn't it, though? So please learn your lesson this time." She giggled. Then she told him she had finished the paperwork for his deliveries. He turned to go back into the Guild Hall, the shouts and clangs of the young adventurers flying at their mentor still sounding behind him.

The girl, his old friend, was standing impatiently next to the cart. When she saw Goblin Slayer, her face lit up. He called to her quietly:

"Shall we go home?"

"Yes, let's!"

The cart was much lighter than it had been in the morning.

When he got back to the farm, he found some sunbaked rocks and began building a stone wall. The foundations of a wall were already in place, but with goblins, you could never be too careful. Even Uncle grudgingly acknowledged the value of the wall, with the logic that it would help keep away wild animals.

Goblin Slayer worked silently until, after the sun had passed its zenith, his old friend came with a basket on her arm. They sat on the grass together, eating sandwiches and drinking cold grape wine for lunch. Time passed at a leisurely pace.

With the wall almost finished and the next day's deliveries loaded on the cart, the sun began to sink below the horizon. His friend said she would get the food ready and went off, leaving him to wander the pastures aimlessly. The grass rustled softly in the early summer breeze.

Above him shone two moons and a sky full of stars. The stars must have already been in their new places for the season, but he couldn't tell. For him, the stars were just a way of orienting himself. When he was younger, his heart still afire with the tales of the old heroes, he had meant to learn the stories of the constellations. But now...

"What is it?" He heard the footsteps faint in the grass behind him. He didn't turn around.

"Hmmm? Dinner's on. But there's no hurry. What are you thinking about?" As he looked up at the stars, she sat down next to him as easily as anything. He thought for a moment then sat down, too. His mail clinked just a little.

"About the future."

"The future?"

"Yes."

"Huh…"

The conversation trailed off, and they fell silent, gazing into the sky. It wasn't an unpleasant silence. It was a silence they welcomed; it was peaceful. The only sounds were the hush of the wind, the babble of the town drifting from far off, the insects, and their own breath. Each seemed to understand what the other wanted to say.

He was human, after all. He would grow old, get hurt. When he was too tired, he would collapse. One day he would reach his limit. If he didn't die first, the day when he could no longer kill goblins would inevitably come.

And what would he do then? He didn't know.

He's weaker than I'd realized, she thought, watching him from the corner of her eye.

"I'm sorry."

The words sprang suddenly, spontaneously, from her lips.

"For what?" He gave an uncharacteristic bob of his head. Perhaps because of his helmet, the gesture seemed oddly broad, childlike.

"No…nothing. It's nothing."

"You're a strange one," he muttered as she giggled.

Is he pouting? It was a small thing, but it hadn't changed since he was young. With that thought in mind, she pulled on his arm.

"Erk…" He found his vision moving, and then the back of his head was resting against something soft. When he looked up, he saw the stars, two moons—and her eyes.

"You'll get oil on yourself."

"I don't mind. These clothes can go in the laundry, and I can go in the bath."

"Is that right?"

"It is." She rested his head on her knees. She stroked his helmet as she leaned near and whispered, "Let's think things over. We can take our time."

"Our time, huh…?"

"Right. We have all the time in the world."

He felt strangely at ease, like a tightly drawn string that had finally loosened. When he closed his eyes, he still knew how she looked though he couldn't see her. Just as she knew how he looked though his face was hidden.

Dinner that night was stew.

§

One lazy day followed another this way for almost a month.

Somewhere, the battle between the adventurers and the evil spirits was growing more heated all the while...

Then, suddenly, it was over.

It was said that a single rookie had followed the guidance of a legendary sword, and at the end of their adventure had slain the demon king. That greenhorn—a young girl, as it happened—thus became the sixteenth Platinum-ranked adventurer in history.

A great celebration was declared in the Capital, and even Goblin Slayer's out-of-the-way city observed some festivities.

Not that any of this had anything to do with him.

He was interested only in the weather, the animals, the crops, and the people around him. Time passed at a leisurely pace. The days had the quality of an afternoon nap.

But all things must end—often too soon.

The end to his idyll appeared in the form of repulsive black blotches on the dew-drenched morning pastures. Trailing mud and excrement across the fields, they were unmistakable: small footprints.

CHAPTER 11

A Party of Adventurers

"I should run? What?" The girl standing in the kitchen making breakfast—Cow Girl—was taken aback by the words. "Why?"

"I found footprints." She understood, if dimly, what that must mean. Someone who didn't know any better might assume they were children's footprints or some faerie prank.

They were small prints, made by bare feet that had been caked in mud and excrement. The feet of someone who thought nothing of trodding down the grass of the pasture.

She knew. She trusted him to know what they were. They both knew the time had finally come—however fervently they had wished that it wouldn't.

"Goblins." He—Goblin Slayer—was always talking about goblins. He stood by the breakfast table in his armor and helmet. It was bizarre, yes, but also the same thing he did every day.

What he did *not* do every day was abandon his inspection of the farm to come and tell her she should flee.

She stopped cooking and looked at her hands. What should she say? She reached for the right words.

"But…you can stop them, can't you?" She wanted him to say something normal in reply. "*Yes*," or "*I can*," or "*That's my intention*." She needed to hear that calm tone.

"No," he said, "I can't." His voice seemed so small. The words sounded like they were being squeezed out of him.

What? An utterance of confusion and surprise escaped her lips. She turned around suddenly and saw him moving slightly, as if he were trembling.

"In a cave, I could take on a hundred goblins and win. Somehow."

Was he afraid?

Him?

Cow Girl's eyes widened in surprise.

Their farm was surrounded by a fence, by a stone wall, barriers he had reinforced himself. There were a few traps, too, set to catch intruding animals.

It was far from perfect. But she knew he had done everything he could to protect them.

As she looked at him, he glanced down once, as if hesitating, but otherwise, he met her eyes squarely. Or at least, he was trying to.

"Our enemy is a lord," he said shortly.

There were ten different sets of footprints. A horde that could decide to attack a well-defended settlement—and then send out ten goblins to scout the place—must have a leader. A hob or a shaman perhaps, but no. On this scale, it had to be…

A goblin lord.

Someone who didn't know better might scoff at the idea. But he *did* know better. He knew exactly what it meant. Most likely, the horde was more than a hundred strong. If scouts had been by, the attack would come today, tomorrow at the latest. There was no time to beg for help from the rulers or the state. Even if there had been—the nobles would never inconvenience themselves for mere goblins.

Goblin Slayer knew all this. Cow Girl did, too.

Because it had been the same ten years before.

"A goblin horde…?" A hundred or more vicious, evil creatures coming right for them?

"I am not a Platinum rank… I'm no hero."

They didn't have the numbers.

They didn't have the strength.

That meant…

"I can't."

That's why.

"*You should run.*

"*Now, while there's still time.*"

Cow Girl moved to stand right in front of him. She stared into his helmet. When she was sure he had nothing more to say, she murmured, "All right."

"You're decided?"

"Yes." She took a breath in and let it out. There were three things in her heart, three things she needed the courage to say.

"...I'm sorry."

Now that she had said the first of them, the rest would be easier.

"I won't leave." She forced her stiff jaws to work into a smile. She wouldn't let him ask why. He knew why. "Because you mean to stay, don't you?"

He said nothing.

"See? I knew it. You go quiet when you get caught. You always have."

"They won't just kill you."

"Yeah. I know," she said, affecting calmness.

His voice sounded cold. He was trying even harder than she was to remain calm. "I was watching."

"...I know." She knew exactly what he meant. Why he fought, why he had kept fighting. She knew all of it.

"The horde may be driven off someday," he said, as if talking to a child. "But don't think you'll be saved. Even if you live that long, your spirit will be broken."

The intent of his words—his attempt to frighten her with the implication *I won't be able to save you, either*—was so blatant she almost laughed.

Not, of course, that he was wrong. He wasn't wrong, and yet...

"So run."

"I said, no." Despite the circumstances, she found she was happy to know he was concerned for her. And she was concerned for him. She had to make him understand that. "I don't want it to happen again." The words came out of their own accord. "There won't be anywhere for you to come home to..." And in her heart she added, *Or me.*

There was no other place she could call home. It had been ten years, and she wasn't even sure she could call this place home. ·

He stared at her distantly, saying nothing. From somewhere in the depths of the darkness of his helmet, he was watching her. Under his gaze, she felt a sudden embarrassment flare up in her. She looked away and turned red; she stared at the ground. Even as she chided herself for being so silly, the words went on, looking for some kind of excuse.

"I-I mean, think about it. Even if we escaped, the animals...the cows, the sheep. They'd all be gone."

He was silent.

"After that, I mean..."

Silent.

"I see." Two whispered words. "Yeah," she murmured back.

"I'm...really sorry. I know I'm being stubborn."

"...Don't make that face. Relax."

She smiled. It was a weak smile, tears beading at the corners of her eyes. She must have looked bad for him to say something like that.

"I will do what I can," he said. And then he—Goblin Slayer—turned away from her.

He shut the door, walked down the hall and outside. He swept his eyes around the farm, carving it into his memory, and then he stepped onto the road to the city.

This was foolishness.

She could have escaped to the city.

Or he could have knocked her out, tied her up, and put her somewhere safe.

Why hadn't he done it? Why hadn't he made her leave?

There was only one reason. He hadn't wanted to.

He didn't want to make her cry again.

"I'm supposed to protect girls..."

"...You."

Goblin Slayer had been talking to himself, and yet there was an answer. Standing next to him, arms folded, was the owner of the farm. He had been listening—or perhaps he had simply overheard.

"You ought to at least say good-bye when you leave," he spat, glaring at Goblin Slayer, who in fact quite agreed with him. Uncle had taken everything on himself, spared them whatever he could.

"I'm sorry. I…"

The owner interrupted Goblin Slayer sharply as he made to apologize. "She's a good girl." He squeezed the words from a pinched mouth on a pained face. "She's grown up so well."

"…Yes."

"So don't you make her cry."

Goblin Slayer was silent, unsure how to respond. If it had been just a matter of saying something, anything, he could have easily made his tongue move and his lips speak.

But after long deliberation, he decided to tell only the truth.

"I will…try."

Sometimes he hated that he couldn't lie. With those murmured words weighing on him, he began to walk.

§

The Adventurers Guild was bustling once more. Full of the sound of the crowd, of equipment being readied, of laughter.

Those who had been away, battling the forces of chaos, had returned. Not everyone, of course, could come back. But no one brought that up.

Some who were not seen again had fallen to monsters in caves or ruins, or on the plains, or in the mountains. Others had moved on to new lands, or had struck it rich and left adventuring, or otherwise retired. No one sought to discover their fates. Those who did not come back would fade slowly from the collective memory until they were truly gone. That was an adventurer's end.

So almost no one looked up when the bell jingled and he walked in, in his cheap leather armor and his helmet, with his small shield strapped to his arm and his ridiculous sword at his hip.

"Oh, Goblin Slayer," Spearman said acidly. "Fancy you being alive."

A few others reacted in a similar vein. They figured he had been off on a long quest or perhaps taking an extended break. The man who showed up every day asking after goblins had become part of the scenery at the Guild.

Goblin Slayer walked in with his usual bold stride, but he did not head for his seat by the wall. He didn't even go to the front desk, but walked directly to the center of the lobby. The adventurers sitting nearby gave him strange looks. They couldn't see his expression behind his helmet.

"Excuse me. Please listen to me." His voice was low and soft, but it carried remarkably well through the ruckus in the Guild Hall. For the first time, most of the people in the hall were looking at him.

"I have a request."

A commotion broke out.

"*Goblin Slayer* has a request?"

"I've never heard him talk before."

"Doesn't he always solo?"

"Naw, he's got some chick with him these days."

"Oh yeah, that slender little thing... Actually, doesn't he have a bunch of party members now?"

"A lizardman and a dwarf or something. And here I thought he only cared about goblins."

"That elf friend of his is almost as cute as that Priestess!"

"Geez, maybe I should get into goblin hunting!"

Goblin Slayer looked at the chattering adventurers one after another. Some he knew by name. Others, not. But he recognized each and every face.

"A goblin horde is coming. They're targeting a farm outside town. Probably tonight. I don't know how many." He spoke calmly to them, these people he knew. The furor among the adventurers grew louder. "But from the number of scouts, I believe there is a lord among them. In other words, at least a hundred goblins."

A hundred goblins! Being led by a lord?

This was no joke. Most adventurers took on goblin slaying as their first quest. Some failed and paid for their failure with their life. Others, though—be it through luck, strength, or who knew what—survived. Many of them were standing there at that moment. They knew in their bones the terror—or rather, frankly, the difficulty—of goblins. Who would willingly fight a host of those creatures? And with a lord present—a goblin who excelled not in strength or magic, but in leadership.

This was no ordinary horde. It was a goblin army.

Even an ignorant beginner would refuse to help. Only Goblin Slayer could happily face down something like that. And even Goblin Slayer, it was clear, was not willing to solo now...

"There's no time. Caves are one thing, but in a pitched battle, I can't do this alone." Goblin Slayer turned, taking in the entire room. "I need your help. Please." Then he lowered his head.

In an instant, whispering voices filled the hall.

"What are you gonna do?"

"What do you think?"

"Goblins, huh...?"

"He should handle it himself."

"Count me out!"

"Me, too. Those things are filthy."

No one said anything directly to Goblin Slayer. He stood with his head bowed, motionless.

"...Hey." When another low voice cut through the crowd, the adventurers set to their tumult again. "How do we know you're right?" It was the spear-wielding adventurer. He fixed Goblin Slayer with an intent gaze.

Goblin Slayer silently raised his head.

"This is the Adventurers Guild," Spearman said, "and we're adventurers."

Goblin Slayer said nothing.

"We don't have to listen to you. You want help, file a quest. Offer a reward, get what I'm saying?" Spearman looked at his fellow adventurers for support.

"He's right!" someone called.

"Yeah, we're adventurers!"

"You want us to risk our lives for free?" The jeers picked up.

Goblin Slayer stood where he was and looked around. Not looking for support, exactly.

At a table deep in the room, High Elf Archer made to stand, her face a furious red, but Dwarf Shaman and Lizard Priest stopped her. Witch sat on a bench, a slippery smile floating on her face. He glanced at the front desk to see Guild Girl vanishing into a back room in a panic. It occurred to him that he was looking for Priestess. Inside his helmet, he closed his eyes.

"Yeah, that guy's right!"

"How about you tell us what you'll pay us to fight a hundred goblins?"

There was no hesitation now. He had given that up ten years ago. Goblin Slayer answered, calmly and clearly:

"Everything."

The Guild Hall fell silent.

Everyone knew what he meant by that word.

"Everything that I have," he said calmly.

If any adventurer fights with me against a hundred goblins, he or she may ask for anything or everything.

Spearman squared his shoulders. "So what if I told you to back off Guild Girl and let me have her?" he asked with a snort.

"She is not mine," Goblin Slayer replied with absolute seriousness. He ignored the whisper that ran through the crowd, calling him unable to take a joke. "All that I have," he said, "that is mine to give. My equipment, my wealth, my knowledge, my time. And…"

"Your life?"

Goblin Slayer nodded yes. "Even my life."

"So if I say *die*, what will you do?" Spearman asked. He sounded exasperated, like he couldn't believe what was happening.

They thought they knew how he would answer. But after a long pause, he said, "No. I cannot do that."

No, of course not. The tension in the air lessened ever so slightly. This guy might not be quite right in the head, but even he was afraid to die.

"If I died, there is someone who would weep over my death. And I have promised not to make that person cry."

Adventurers who had been listening with bated breath looked at one another.

"So my life is not mine to give, either."

Spearman swallowed heavily. He glared at Goblin Slayer. At the metal helmet that stood between him and the expression behind it. He met Goblin Slayer's eyes in spite of the mask.

"I don't know what the hell you're thinking."

Goblin Slayer said nothing.

"I get that you're serious."

"Yes." He nodded quietly. "I am."

"Damn it all!" Spearman said, tearing at his hair. He began to pace back and forth in front of Goblin Slayer, tapping the floor with the butt of his spear. The agonized moment stretched on and on. Finally, Spearman heaved a sigh and said in a voice heavy with resignation, "What would I do with your life, anyway? ...But you owe me one hell of a drink."

He pounded his fist once against Goblin Slayer's leather chest plate.

Goblin Slayer tottered. The steel helmet looked vacantly at Spearman.

Spearman stared back at him. *Got a problem?* "A Silver-ranked adventurer just took on your goblin-slaying quest. At market rate, no less. You ought to be grateful."

"...I am." Goblin Slayer nodded firmly. "Pardon me. Thank you."

"Save it for after we've slain some goblins." Spearman's eyes widened a bit, and he scratched his cheek uncomfortably. He'd never thought the day would come when he would hear "thank you" from this man.

"I-I'm with you, too!" A clear voice rang through the Guild Hall. Everyone turned to look at an elven archer who had kicked over her chair as she stood. She quailed under their gaze, her long ears trembling. "I...I'll slay those goblins with you." Her courage seemed to well up then, and she walked straight across the room to Goblin Slayer and stuck a finger in his chest. "So...so next time, you have to come on an adventure with me! I found some...some ruins."

"Very well." Goblin Slayer nodded immediately. The elf's ears stood straight up. "If I survive, I will join you."

"Gosh, you didn't have to say that," the elf huffed, glaring at the helmet. She spun around. "You're coming, too, right?"

The dwarf answered first, sighing as he stroked his beard with a touch of annoyance. "Guess I've no choice. But I won't be bought off with one drink, Beard-cutter. You'd better bring me a whole barrel!"

"You'll have it," Goblin Slayer said.

"Right, then!" the dwarf exclaimed happily. "And...supposin' I could join you on your adventure, long-ears?"

"Of course! We're party members, aren't we?" The elf laughed, and after a second, the dwarf joined in.

"Let it never be said that I would leave my companions behind." The lizardman stood slowly. He touched the tip of his nose with his tongue. "Nor that I would turn down a friend in need. But speaking of rewards..."

"Cheese?"

"Precisely. Ah, I can taste it now!"

"It is not mine. But it is made on the farm that's being targeted."

"Indeed? All the more reason to destroy those bottom-feeding beasts!" The lizardman's eyes rolled, and he joined his palms toward Goblin Slayer. The latter understood that this was a form of lizardman humor.

So four adventurers gathered around Goblin Slayer.

He didn't see Priestess anywhere.

"So, we have five..."

"No. Six." Witch stood with a rustling sound. She walked over and stood beside Spearman, hips swaying all the way. "It might well be seven...though, I can't, be sure," she said meaningfully; then she drew a long pipe out from her bosom. "*Inflammarae.*" She spun the pipe around, stuffed some tobacco in it, then lit it with a tap of her finger and took a long breath. The sweet-smelling smoke wafted around the Guild Hall.

The remaining adventurers babbled excitedly. It wasn't that they wanted to abandon the farm to destruction. Many of them simply weren't ready to risk their lives for a pittance. And who could blame them? Everyone values their own lives.

They just needed one more push...

"The Guild is— The Guild is offering a quest, too!"

That push came from an energetic voice. Guild Girl came bounding out of the back room clutching a sheaf of paper. She was breathing hard, her face red, her braids bouncing wildly up and down.

She began to pile the paper on the front desk. "There is a reward of one gold coin for each goblin you slay. Now's your chance, adventurers!"

The crowd gave a collective stir. It was of course the Guild that would provide the money for the reward. The ability to work on a large scale was one of the advantages of such an organization.

There was no telling how hard Guild Girl had fought to convince her superiors that this was a good idea.

"Feh. Guess I'm in, then." An adventurer—the heavily armored warrior—gave his chair a little kick as he stood and took one of the sheets of paper. Knight, seated beside him, looked up at him in surprise.

"You're going?"

"I'm no fan of Goblin Slayer, but hey…money is money."

Knight got a devilish grin on her delicate face. "I can't abide liars. You ought to just admit it's because he's the one who drove the goblins out of your hometown."

"Hey, keep it to yourself, woman! Anyway, I'll still get a gold coin per goblin."

Me, too. Yeah, count me in. I owe that guy. One by one, the murmurs started; people rose to their feet.

"And what about you? I thought you hated his guts."

"I aspire to be a paladin. When someone asks for help, I'm bound to offer it," Knight said with a smirk, to which Warrior, in armor, responded with a shrug and a laugh.

"Aw, well. If you two are going, I guess we're coming along."

"We are?"

"Now, now, of course we must help!"

Despite a little arguing, the rest of the armored warrior's party stood up.

"Hey…"

"What?"

Watching them, the greenhorn warrior they had sparred with many days ago called to the young Cleric.

"I've still never been goblin slaying."

"…I guess not. They say it's dangerous."

"But…I've got to try it sometime, right?"

"…You're hopeless," she said. *But…if you must.* And the boy held out his hand to her.

Somebody watching them gave a short sigh. "I became an adventurer the same day he did. Guess this is what you'd call fate."

"If I didn't hear that voice asking after goblins every day, it wouldn't feel right."

"I agree. He's kind of a…fixture here—an institution, you know?"

"I hate having him around. But…I'd hate not having him around even more."

"I was just looking for a way to get some cash. One goblin, one gold, huh? Not bad."

"In all my life, I've never seen such a weird quest giver," someone muttered. Someone else nodded. One after another, adventurers rose.

Yes, they were adventurers.

They had dreams in their hearts. They had principles. They had ambitions. They wanted to fight for people.

Maybe they didn't have the courage to step forward. But they'd been given that little push. There was no more reason to hesitate.

Goblin slaying? Fine. That was their job. If there was a quest, they would take it.

Someone raised their sword in the air and cried, "We ain't party members, and we ain't friends—but we're adventurers!" Others joined the shout. Those who did not carry swords raised staves, spears, axes, bows, fists.

There were beginners. Veterans. Warriors, wizards, clerics, and rogues. There were humans, elves, dwarves, lizardmen, and rheas. The adventurers gathered in the Guild Hall filled the air with their voices, pounded the floor with their feet.

Goblin Slayer, embraced by their shouts, surveyed the room. His eyes met Guild Girl's. She was sweating a little, but she gave him a puckish wink. Goblin Slayer bowed his head to her. He felt it was the least he could do.

"That worked out well." There was a little giggle.

He turned around and saw, standing close as a shadow, Priestess.

Of course she was there. How could she not be?

"...Yes. It did." Goblin Slayer nodded.

That day, perhaps for the first time, there was no shortage of adventurers ready to take on a goblin quest.

CHAPTER 12

OVER THE GOBLINS' HILL

It was the start of a long night.

"GRARARARARARA! GRARARARA!!"

Seeing the moon at the top of the sky—"high noon" for his people—the goblin lord gave his orders.

His words were conveyed in an instant by a clamor of growling voices, and the goblin army began to advance. Hidden in a field of grass as tall as they were, they raised their shields as they came to their feet. The goblins called them "meat shields": boards to which captured women and children had been tied. In all, ten naked prisoners were held before the army. They periodically moaned, or spasmed, or twitched uncomprehendingly.

The goblins, for their part, had already had plenty of sport with these prisoners. Whether the meat shield lived or died mattered nothing to them. What mattered was that this would cause opposing adventurers to falter when launching an arrow or a spell. By contrast, if an adventurer had captured a goblin and used him in the same way, no other goblin would have hesitated to shoot straight through him. True, he might have been angry about having to kill his fellow goblin, but it would only be all the more motivation to tear his enemy apart.

The goblin lord cackled at the thought of what fools adventurers were.

At the edge of sight, they could make out the lights of the farm. The city could just be seen farther beyond.

There were adventurers in the city. *Adventurers!* A filthy word for filthy creatures.

The goblin lord came to a snap decision. He would take each adventurer and pound them full of stakes until they died. Maybe by the end, they would repent of all they had done to his kind.

Just like the adventurers who had attacked his nest—his home—and had abandoned him in the wilderness because he was so young.

They would start with the farm. Steal the cattle and sheep to fill their bellies. Take the girl for their own to increase their numbers.

The farm would make a convenient beachhead to attack the city, slaughter the adventurers, and further bolster their ranks. Then, finally, they would turn toward the human Capital, raze it, and raise up a goblin kingdom in its place!

That day was still a dream, but the plan in the goblin lord's mind was quite real.

The rank and file below him could not make sense of it. But they had their anger, and their hatred, and their lust roiling within them. Reconnaissance of the farm had revealed the presence not just of fresh meat, but of a young girl.

They moved ardently through the grass, which rustled as they went. Finally, the lights of the farm were near. In moments, the attack would begin.

Then it happened.

"GRUUU?"

A sweet-smelling mist drifted over the field. One of the shield bearers at the front of the army was pulled into it, and a moment later, he reemerged, facing quite the other direction, and collapsed on the ground. The other shield bearers began to fall one by one. In the instant it took the startled goblin lord to blink, dark forms leaped from the shadows around the farm's wall.

Adventurers! This is magic!

"GAAAUU!!" The lord gave a high screech.

"GAUGARRR!!" A goblin shaman shouted something and waved his staff. A bolt of lightning shot out and struck an adventurer in the chest. But as the one adventurer fell, the others rapidly closed distance with the goblins and grabbed the meat shields. They ignored the enemy entirely, instead retreating as quickly as they had come. The shaman waved his staff again and chanted, hoping to hit one of the fleeing adventurers.

"GAAA?!"

An arrow made from a branch pierced his chest. His mouth worked open and closed for a moment, and then he fell faceup on the grass, dead.

Thanks to their excellent night vision, the goblins soon located the source of the shot.

Up in one of the trees on the farm—an elf. An elf was shooting at them!

Goblin archers rushed to return fire from their short bows, but the elf only snorted and leaped into the brush.

The adventurers carrying the meat shields made it over the wall, and in exchange, a group of their armed companions appeared. They kept low as they raced toward the goblins, accompanied by the clatter of their armor.

"GORRRRR!!"

The goblin lord hurriedly shouted at his troops to counterattack, but they were not quite conscious enough to obey him. The Stupor spell was working its magic on them, and one after another, they were struck down by arrows with the haze still in their minds.

"So those are their 'shields.' Twisted creatures," the elf said, disgust playing across her face. She dashed across the field, firing arrows like the wind. She could shoot as easily as she could breathe. She could have hit her targets with her eyes shut. Her arrows reaped goblins like a scythe through wheat.

She had not actually killed that many of the foe. But she couldn't go on forever.

"I took out their spell caster!"

"All right, you louts! Time to earn your pay!"

"Ha-haaa! Lookit our gold marching right toward us!"

The adventurers made contact with the enemy before the confused goblin army could reform itself.

Now neither side could use spells that might catch their own allies in the effect—the adventurers naturally, but even the goblins had some sense of risk and reward. They had no qualms about using their companions as shields, but they had to be careful that the number of shields available didn't get too low. And anyway, even when it came to using spells, goblins were still goblins. They were cowardly and cruel.

Thus, the battle began.

The ring of swordplay resounded. The smell of blood was everywhere upon the night-wrapped plain. Screams, wails, war cries. Amid the clamor, silhouettes—adventurers, goblins—could be seen vanishing one by one as the combatants fell.

"Gods, there're enough goblins here to put you off 'em for life!" Spearman roared with laughter as he knocked down foe after foe.

As each monster tumbled to the ground, Lizard Priest leaped upon them and struck the finishing blow. "Indeed, even milord Goblin Slayer was at his wits' end..." He made his palms-together gesture and drew his fang-sword. There were still many goblins to slay.

"Not that, I mind, but for your own sake...stay within, my Deflect Missile spell, won't you?" Witch stood nearby, staff in hand and letting off spell after spell, her generous chest heaving as she gulped in breath.

Nearby, Dwarf Shaman had used Stupor as many times as he was able and had resorted to his sling. "Bury me, Beard-cutter was right that no one could handle this lot alone!" He fired a stone that traced a perfect line from his sling to a goblin's head. "Goodness," he said, "around here you hardly even need to ai— Wha—?!"

Dwarf Shaman squinted. High Elf Archer noticed immediately and shouted, "What is it, dwarf?"

"Riders, long-ears! Mounted goblins on the way!"

Howls echoed across the moons-lit field. Goblins straddling huge gray wolves and swinging swords came cleaving through the darkness.

"I'll shoot them from here! Hold them off!"

"Right! Spear wall, don't let them through!" At Spearman's orders, nearby adventurers stood shoulder to shoulder and thrust out their weapons. The wolves came on as if oblivious to the hail of arrows raining down on them. Adventurers gladly thrust their blades into the bellies of the beasts.

There was a howl and cry, a piercing scream.

"Errraggghh!"

One adventurer had been worsted by a charging rider and found a wolf at their throat. Many of the animals, though, succumbed to the adventurers' attacks, throwing the goblins from their backs.

"Chaaaaaarge!" The lizardman led with a great bellow and flew to finish off the toppled riders. Warrior priest that he was, from time to time, he cried out shrilly in what might have been a prayer of the lizardmen.

All in all, the adventurers were winning quite handily.

In general, in a straight contest between an adventurer and a goblin, the adventurer will normally come out on top, so long as ill luck does not intervene. And what was more...

Goblin Slayer said: "Set ambushes. They specialize in surprise attacks but never expect to be ambushed themselves."

He said: "Take a low stance. Aim for the legs. They're small, but they can't fly."

He said: "They will certainly have meat shields. Cast sleep spells, then use that moment to rescue the hostages."

He said: "Even if you think you can kill them while rescuing the shields, don't. If they wake up, it will only be trouble."

He said: "Don't use attack magic. Save your spells for other things."

He said: "Swords, spears, arrows, axes, any kind of weapon can be used to kill them. What you can't do with a weapon, do with magic."

He said: "Take out their spell casters first."

He said: "Don't let them get behind you. Always keep moving. Small movements with your weapon. Conserve your strength."

He said...

The other adventurers were frankly astonished at the amount of knowledge Goblin Slayer imparted to them.

Adventurers were not soldiers, but they were no strangers to strategy. Yet they were not used to taking such care against goblins. Experienced and fledgling adventurers alike saw goblins as insignificant foes.

"Man! Not only do I get to make some serious cash; I get to impress my girl!" With these tactics in hand, goblins were simple to deal with so long as they could be forced into one-on-one battles. Spearman

and the other warriors thrust their weapons left and right, everywhere finding a goblin to kill.

Deep within the enemy ranks, however, they could see a vast form tower up, silhouetted against the moon.

"There it is! A hob— Wait, is it?"

"GURAURAURAURAURAUUUU!!"

The great roar rolled across the bloodied battlefield.

The creature was so large it could have been taken for an ogre. It held a club stained with blood and brains. A goblin champion.

A goblin, yes, but one so powerful it could single-handedly turn the tide of battle.

Far be it for any adventurer, though, to back down from a challenge just because it was twice their size and carried a big stick.

"Ahhh, there's the big one! I was getting tired of these small-fries!" The heavy warrior was the first to dive at the champion, with his weapon on his shoulder and a wild laugh on his lips. Rolling her eyes, Knight followed him, with her shield up.

"Just when I was busy counting up how many goblin heads I'd collected," she said.

"Count 'em later! Fight now!"

"You warriors have such one-track minds." With this banter, they happily jumped into battle against the new foe.

All over the field, weapons rang against one another, and blood spurted into the air.

"And where is our fearless leader in all this?" Spearman asked, as he stopped to wipe the point of his spear on a wolf's fur. His breath was growing ragged.

Across the field, a new dark mass had appeared.

Goblin reinforcements. There was no time to rest. He held his spear close and made ready.

"Oh, I think, you know, the answer, to that," Witch whispered in a honeyed voice, as she took a long draw on her pipe and slowly let out her breath. Sweet-smelling pink vapor floated on the wind, and every goblin who breathed it in found their senses dulled. In the distance, the reinforcements began to move more slowly as well.

"Obviously," High Elf Archer said with a laugh, firing at the stupe-fied foes. "He's gone to slay goblins."

§

How could this have happened?!

The goblin lord ran so quickly he was almost stumbling. As soon as he had realized there was no chance of victory, he had fled the battlefield. Behind him, he could hear weapons clanging, screams, the sound of spells reverberating.

Some of those screams must have been adventurers. But most were goblins.

This was supposed to be a surprise attack to establish a foothold in the area. And yet...

It is we who take! So how did this happen?!

His horde was lost. With his forces checked, there was no point in hanging around.

As long as he survived, that was all that mattered.

He would go back to the nest, use the captured women there to build up his ranks.

Just like before.

The goblin lord was a Wanderer, the lone survivor of a nest destroyed by adventurers. Now, he lived only to slay adventurers.

It's not so hard.

His first victim had been the woman who had spared him "because he was just a child." She had become food for him as soon as she turned her back.

He had learned then that if you hit an adventurer hard enough on the head with a rock, they became quite pliant. When he found out a club was more effective still, he used that. Then, he had learned to use weapons and wear armor. From the way adventurers formed their parties, he gleaned the best ways to lead a horde.

His long days of drifting had trained his body and mind until he was a match even for a human warrior.

This would be the same.

Beneath the two moons, the lord turned away from the battle and ran for his life.

Through the grass, kicking up earth, toward the forest. Into the forest. There was a cave there. His nest.

He had failed. But so long as he lived, there would be another chance.

He would learn, and replenish his ranks, and the next time would be better. The next time—

"I knew you would come here."

A calm, cold, almost mechanical voice caught him. Unthinkingly, the goblin lord stopped in his tracks. He readied the battle-ax he held in his hand.

His eyes could pick out the figure standing before him in the dark. It was an adventurer in cheap leather armor and a steel helmet. A small shield bound to his left arm, and in his right hand, a sword almost too long to wield. He was spattered with blood from killing, standing in a nauseating puddle of it.

"Fool. I see both of us used our armies as decoys."

The lord could speak the common tongue, though he despised it. He did not know who this adventurer was. But it was all too clear what had happened.

"Your home is no more."

"ORGRRRRRR!!"

The lord gave an earsplitting yell and leaped at Goblin Slayer. The lord brought his ax down in an arc, meaning to split the adventurer's skull open, but Goblin Slayer blocked the blow with his shield. There was a noise of rending metal.

Goblin Slayer gave a great shake of the shield and pushed the ax aside, then made a sharp thrust with his sword.

"Hrm!" he muttered.

The tip of his sword struck the lord in the chest but made only a dull thump. The goblin was wearing a chest plate.

Goblin Slayer was unfazed but frozen for a second, and in that moment, the ax came at him from the side.

An instant's decision. He flung himself to the side, rolling to avoid the blow. He rose to one knee, panting.

©Noboru Kanna

"…"

Goblin Slayer stood and rolled his sword slowly in his hand, holding his shield before him.

"GRRRR…"

The lord made a sound of disgust and gripped his battle-ax with both hands.

The gulf between them in strength and armament was immense.

His wounds from before. The month of recuperating. He had needed that time to heal, and yet…

Goblin Slayer was acutely aware that his skills had dulled. It would not be a problem, however. He would not let it be a problem. There was a goblin in front of him. That was all he needed.

"…!"

Goblin Slayer loosed himself like an arrow upon his foe.

He moved in a low stance; with his left hand, he grabbed a fistful of grass, cut it free, and threw it at the goblin lord.

In the second it took the lord to wave away the cloud of grass, Goblin Slayer thrust with his sword.

Blood flying, a scream.

"GARUARAARARAA?!" The lord swung his battle-ax in a frenzy, bleeding from the forehead. Before an observer could have clucked their tongue, a strike connected with Goblin Slayer.

He felt himself floating through the air—and then landing painfully on the ground.

"Oof! Agh…" The hard earth met his back, forcing the air from his lungs. He saw his shield had been split nearly in half.

His skills may have rusted, but his muscles still remembered their part. The shield he had instinctively raised had saved his life again.

"They're no good at frontal attacks…," he muttered, rising, supporting himself on his sword.

"GAROOOO!!"

The goblin lord was not going to miss his chance. He came charging through the grass.

Goblin Slayer gave a small nod. He held his sword high, raised his battered shield, and faced the lord head-on.

An instant later, he was dashing at the enemy.

The goblin lord's battle-ax came whistling through the air. Goblin Slayer held up his shield to meet it and thrust with his sword.

Impact.

The ax split the shield in two and bit deep into Goblin Slayer's arm. The adventurer went flying once more.

But in the same moment, his sword had sliced into the goblin's belly, which now gushed blood onto the dark field.

"GAU…"

But the wound was hardly fatal. The lord frowned angrily.

"Ugh, hrk…?!" Goblin Slayer scrambled to get up out of the dirt. But he couldn't stand. He tried to use his sword to heft himself up, but it was broken.

"GURRR…" The goblin sounded almost bored. At least he would have his revenge for his fallen troops. He would cut off this man's hands and feet, tie him to a post, and torture him to death. As he envisioned this grim future, the goblin lord began to cackle, then stalked slowly toward his prey.

He gave a vicious kick to Goblin Slayer's motionless helmet.

Silence.

The lord was not pleased. Prey were supposed to cower at the moment of death.

But so be it.

Death would put an end to this. To everything. Perhaps tonight he would have to be content with that.

The goblin lord raised his battle-ax slowly.

Crack.

The next second, the ax was thrown backward.

"GAU…?"

Had he hit a tree root or something? The lord looked back in frustration, but there was nothing there. The nearest trees stood some distance away.

"GA, RRR…?!"

This time as he attempted to bring his weapon down, the lord found the ax would not move at all. No—it was his own body that was not answering his commands. His bones creaked like something was pushing against him. Like he was trapped between two invisible walls.

"GA, GAO…?!"

The lord's eyes swept back and forth; he could not even fidget.

What was…? What was going on…?!

"O Earth Mother, abounding in mercy, by the power of the land grant safety to we who are weak…"

The answer to his question came in the form of a miraculously clear voice intoning a prayer.

A beautiful young woman walked out of the nearby copse. Sweat beaded on her forehead, and in her trembling hands was a sounding staff.

A young priestess praying fervently to the Earth Mother.

This is her doing!

"GAAAAUUAUAUAUAUAAA!!"

The goblin lord howled every vile threat he knew at her. He would tear off her limbs and make her eat them! No, he would pound a spike so far up her ass it came out her mouth! He would break her fingers into tiny pieces one by one, burn her face until no one could recognize her…

She looked so frail. Surely a bit of intimidation was all it would take to scare her off…

"…!"

But he was wrong.

Face pale, biting her lip, Priestess still held out her quaking staff.

The lord began to worry.

"GA…RO…?"

Perhaps this girl was not quite what she seemed.

A change of tactics, then. The lord put on his most pitiful expression and begged for forgiveness. He would never do such a thing again. He had been wrong, so wrong. He would go and live quietly in the woods, never see a human village again. Please forgive him. Please.

He babbled on in his pathetic version of the common tongue. Had it been possible, he might have thrown himself at her feet.

It wouldn't be the first time he had convinced an adventurer to spare his life through a show of repentance.

The first time was long before he had become a lord—in fact, he had still been a child. Come to think of it, that adventurer had been a woman, too. *"All right,"* she had said, *"but you must never do this sort of thing again.*" He had agreed eagerly. And then, of course, murdered her as soon as she turned around.

He took a black joy from his memory of that woman begging for help as he stabbed her to death. She had thought she was strong.

If he could live now, there would yet be time to plot his revenge.

And first of all, I will take this girl!

"As if I would ever let you." A cold voice rang out, bit into him.

"GA, RR...?!"

The voice sent ice through his veins like a wind from the bowels of the earth.

Goblin Slayer came slowly to his feet.

His left arm dribbled blood. In his left hand, he held his cloven shield. In his right, his broken sword.

He strode boldly toward the goblin lord. He pushed his sword into the side of the paralyzed goblin's neck.

"GA...GO...?!"

The broken weapon could not cut or pierce.

But it could crush. The creature gibbered nonsensically as the blade pressed on his windpipe.

"A lord? Ridiculous." The lord tried desperately to struggle.

"You're a goblin."

The goblin opened his mouth, fighting for air.

"Just a filthy..."

But he could do nothing.

"...worthless goblin."

The lord's face changed color, and his tongue lolled out. Spittle foamed at the edge of his mouth; his eyes rolled upward in his head.

"And I..."

As the lord felt consciousness slipping away, a question rose in his vanishing mind.

What? What are you?

"...am Goblin Slayer!"

The creature's eyes remained rolled at the back of his head. The goblin who would be king spasmed once, twice, and died. There was a long silence.

"That's one...goblin head..."

Goblin Slayer's sword dropped from his hand even as the words fell from his lips. Then he slumped forward as though his strings had been cut.

Priestess tossed her staff aside, rushed forward, and caught him. "Goblin Slayer, sir!" He was so heavy in her thin arms, covered in leather and metal and mud and blood.

A moment later, the Protection miracle faded, and the goblin lord's body collapsed next to Goblin Slayer's. Priestess did not glance at it but looked over Goblin Slayer's wounds. There was a deep gash in his left arm. In the worst case, it might go all the way down to the bone.

"Please...don't do these foolish things..."

"...Urgh..."

She put his groan out of mind as she pressed her palms to his wound, ignoring the blood that stained her hands.

"O Earth Mother, abounding in mercy, lay your revered hand upon your child's wounds..."

The prayer was soul-effacing, intent, and heartfelt.

What happened on that first adventure...? I never want it to happen again...

The Earth Mother graciously heard her supplication and touched Goblin Slayer's arm with her shining finger. This was how Priestess used her remaining miracle.

He had told her that he would distract the goblin lord while she used Protection.

She was no longer disturbed by the thought of using two Protection miracles in tandem, not to guard her target, but to trap it. But she had not added the third Protection miracle as he had instructed.

Perhaps it was a revelation that kept her from exhausting her miracles. For if she had, the life of this man—this strange, stubborn, serious man—would have ended here.

"...Grief. I told you already..."

"Goblin Slayer, sir!"

To the rough voice that reached up to her, she answered with tears in her eyes.

"...Foolishness isn't what wins battles."

Goblin Slayer sat up painfully. Priestess helped him as best she could, wedging herself under his arm. He had been almost too heavy to hold. Now she tried to help lift him to his feet. Struggling to grasp him with her willowy, beautiful arms, Priestess supported him on her shoulder and stood.

"You may…say that…"

"…"

"…But I think…you need to be more careful…!"

"I do?"

She was silent.

"…I'm sorry."

Sniffling, sobbing, Priestess shook her head vehemently.

Step by tearstained step, she began walking slowly, certainly forward.

Taking care to take as much of his weight off her as he could, Goblin Slayer said calmly, "It was because I trust you."

Priestess smiled through the tears that ran down her cheeks. "…You really are hopeless, aren't you?"

She thought of her companions who had died on their first adventure together. She thought of the adventurers who were bleeding and dying even now. She thought of the goblins that had been killed. She thought of the goblin lord who had died before her eyes.

As all these things spun in her mind, she became aware of the weight of the man leaning on her. It was all she could do to hold him up with her exhausted body.

She advanced one laborious step at a time, barely moving. The sounds of battle were far away, and the lights of the city farther still.

But with every step, her heart was glad.

CHAPTER 13

THE FATE OF AN ADVENTURER

"To our victory, to the farm, to our city, to our adventurers—"

High Elf Archer looked around at all her allies who had gathered at the Guild Hall, each with their various injuries.

"—and to the weirdo who's always on about goblins! Cheers!"

A great shout went up from the crowd, and everyone drained their cup. This was the fifth or sixth toast, but nobody minded. They had come to the Guild Hall practically before the blood was dry from the battle, and they were giddy with victory.

And what a victory it was.

A hundred goblins destroyed. The goblins had had shamans, champions, and more on their side, and still they had been no match for the adventurers.

Of course, the adventurers had not escaped unscathed. There were dead and wounded. There are always those caught by ill luck. So the commotion here was not only in celebration of victory but in remembrance of fallen friends. Everyone who took up adventuring knew that tomorrow it could be them.

When the battle ended, Cow Girl and her uncle were caught up in the festivities as well, and the revelry quickly grew and spread.

He—as always—sat on a bench in the corner near the wall.

His left arm was bandaged to his chest, but the pain seemed to have gone. He watched the party in the reflection on the shining surface of a single gold coin.

Dwarf Shaman had produced his personal stash of fire wine and was sharing it around. More than one rookie found themselves three sheets to the wind before they'd finished an entire cup.

Next to the dwarf, a Dragontooth Warrior, under the control of Lizard Priest, performed a bizarre dance to acclaim.

Guild Girl was running around like an excited puppy. When Spearman reached out to her, Witch gave him a sharp rap with her pipe.

"Barkeep! I'm a rich woman tonight! Keep 'em coming!"

"Meat! Bring meat! Well marbled!"

"Didn't you say you'd date me? Huh? What about going to meet my parents back home…?!"

"Yow! How many drinks have you had?"

"All riiiight! Join me in a drink—today of all days!"

"Oh, how about an antidote to protect against hangovers?"

"…One, please."

He squinted a little.

He had cleared out the entire goblin nest, but of the army proper, he had killed only the lord.

Hence his reward: one gold coin.

He pressed the coin into the palm of Priestess, who sat next to him. Earlier, she had been smiling brightly, but as the party wore on, she rested her head on his shoulder and was now breathing shallowly in sleep.

"She must have fought really hard."

From the other side of the young girl, she—Cow Girl—stroked Priestess's hair. She rubbed a bit of dirt from Priestess's cheek in a gesture that reminded him of an older sister taking care of her younger sibling. "She's just a girl. Don't make her overwork herself, all right?"

"Yes." He nodded calmly. Cow Girl pinched up her lips.

"Aren't you in a kind mood." She paused. "Did something happen?"

"It's nothing," he said with a slight shake of his head.

"Just like always."

"…Really?"

The two of them fell silent, watching the adventurers. The gathered victors drank and ate and laughed and made merry. The wounded and the unharmed alike. Those who had especially distinguished themselves and those who hadn't. All the survivors enjoying what they had earned by this adventure.

"...Thank you," she whispered to him.

"For what?"

"Saving us."

"...I didn't do anything," he said brusquely.

Silence returned between them. It wasn't uncomfortable. Each of them knew what the other was thinking.

"It isn't..."

"Hmm?" She cocked her head at his subdued whisper.

"It isn't over yet..."

"Maybe. But this is something."

She waited for him to reply.

He thought and thought, and then said slowly, with hesitation, "I suppose...I think I want...to become an adventurer."

"Yeah?"

To her, he sounded like he was ten years old again. But unlike when she'd been eight, this time she could answer with a smile and an encouraging nod. "I'm sure you can do it."

"Are you?"

"Yeah, I am."

It might not be until that far-off day when there were no more goblins, but...

"Mm...ha...aah?" At that moment, Priestess stirred. Her eyelids fluttered open. "Huh, wha—?! D-did I fall asleep...?" she asked, her face bright red. At the sight of her, she—Cow Girl—giggled.

"Ha-ha-ha. Everyone fought so hard today. We can't blame you for wanting a little nap."

"Oh, ahh, um...I'm s-sorry..."

"I don't mind."

"All right. I have to go say thanks to a few people." With one more affectionate stroke of Priestess's hair, Cow Girl stood up. The "Take it easy *today*" that she tossed out as she went elicited a nod from him and a blush and a look at the ground from Priestess.

"...Are you all right, not joining the others?"

Priestess shook her head. "I'm fine." She paused. "I'm…enjoying myself."

No, it's not all right… I don't know why, but this can't go on…

Suddenly, Priestess clapped her hands. This was something else she had learned from Goblin Slayer: much better to act in the moment than to come up with the perfect strategy after the fact.

"Wh-what about you, Goblin Slayer, sir? Are you all right?"

"With what?"

"With…money or…anything?"

"No problems." It was a blunt change of topic, and whether or not Goblin Slayer recognized that, he nodded. "I have compensated everyone as we agreed."

She gave him a questioning look.

"I bought a round of drinks."

"Ah." Priestess unconsciously put a hand to her mouth. Her gaze had just then settled on Spearman, who was popping the cork on another bottle of fine wine. Next to him, Witch was savoring her first cup of top-class wine.

He must know, right? Surely. Probably.

"…You're a sharp one, aren't you?"

"The market has decided that goblin slaying does not pay much."

"And is that okay?"

"I think so.

"Anyway," he muttered, "the Guild is paying the actual reward." It didn't cost him anything.

She looked at him with half-closed eyes. He really didn't seem bothered. Of course, Priestess wasn't really being serious, either. It was just banter. She felt like she was floating along. Her heart leaped. Blood rushed through her body.

"Goblin Slayer, sir…"

"Yes?"

"Why didn't you…? I mean, why not post a regular quest?"

Were those theatrics at the Guild really necessary? Wouldn't it have been enough to post a quest normally? Those were the questions in her mind.

Goblin Slayer was silent.

"If you don't want to answer, that's…that's fine…," she added hurriedly.

The silence stretched on a moment longer.

"There was no important reason," he said with a shake of his head. "Only…when it happened to me, no one came."

He looked out at the crowd of well-liquored adventurers. Those who had rushed to join him, those who had risked their lives to slay goblins.

And those who hadn't come back here, who had died.

"It was possible no one would come this time, either. There are no promises. Only luck."

That was his only reason. He muttered: "And because, I hear, I'm a 'weirdo.'"

Then the steel helmet was silent once more. Priestess sighed.

This guy really was hopeless.

So she said to him: "You're wrong. If you ask for my help, I'll help you."

"Don't be stupid."

"Not just me, either. All the adventurers in this city—all of them."

In her heart of hearts, she sighed. He really was absolutely hopeless.

"Next time, too. And the time after that. Whenever you need help, I'll be here. We'll be here."

Her heart of hearts was where she found her next words as well.

"So…so luck has nothing to do with it." She smiled then, a bashful grin that emerged like a blooming flower.

"Is that so?" he muttered, and she said, "Yes, it is," puffing out her chest a little.

Now…now she could say it, couldn't she?

Her heart pounded in her chest. She clenched her fists and let out a breath.

"Say, Goblin Slayer, sir…"

She must be drunk. The drink had made her do it. Yes, that would serve for an excuse.

"I know it's a bit late, but…could I ask for a reward, too?"

"What reward?"

Please, oh please, Earth Mother, give me courage…

The courage to say the words that would tell him what she wanted.

She breathed in, out. She looked straight at him.

"Please, let me see your face. Your real face."

He said nothing for a very long moment.

But then he sighed, almost in resignation, and put his hands on his helmet.

He released the latches and removed the helm, and after that long battle, there he was, under the lights of the hall.

Priestess laughed quietly and nodded, making no effort to hide her red cheeks.

"I think you look...even braver this way."

"Do you?"

It was at that moment, as she nodded, that a scream pierced the air.

"Ahhhh!! Orcbolg, you took off your helmet?! No fair! I've never gotten a chance to see your face!" High Elf Archer's face was bright red. She was pointing a finger at him, and her ears were trembling wildly.

"What?!"

"What did you say?!"

None of the other adventurers missed what had happened, either. After all, their acute powers of perception were a key to their survival.

Naturally, the revelers pressed in to see him, still holding their drinks, their food.

"Wha-wha-whaaa—? Amazing! What an opportunity!"

"You think? I guess so. He probably only takes that helmet off when he's asleep or when it breaks..."

"Oh-ho! Now, that is how a warrior should look!"

"I'd expect no less from you, Beard-cutter. You've a good look about you."

"Huh...? I feel like I know him from somewhere... Pfft! Good grief. I can't stand that face."

"Hee-hee. I knew, you must be...quite handsome, under that armor."

"Wait, that's Goblin Slayer's face?!"

"Hey, bring me the books we kept on those bets!"

"...Does this mean those evil spirits are coming back tomorrow?"

"Dang, and here I'd bet everything that was a woman in that armor!"

"I thought he must be a goblin himself..."

"Heyyy, did anyone guess right? Come here and collect!"

©Noboru Kannatuki

He was jostled by adopted family, friends, and comrades in arms—people he knew and people he'd never met—all trying to get a better look at him. Next to him, Priestess, who was caught up with him in the press of bodies, was distraught. She looked at him for help.

It was loud, lively, unrestrained.

Tomorrow, things would probably go back to normal.

Nothing would have changed. Nothing at all.

Except...

"Next time, too. And the time after that. Whenever you need help, I'll be here. We'll be here."

"Is that so...?"

"So...so luck has nothing to do with it."

"I hope...that is true."

And with those words, ever so faintly, he smiled.

§

Once upon a time, in the days when the stars shone far fewer in the sky than they do now...

The gods of light and order and destiny vied with the gods of darkness and chaos and chance to see who would control the world. This struggle took place not in battle, but with a roll of the dice.

Or rather, many, many rolls. Again and again and again they rolled the dice.

And there were victories and there were defeats, but there was no resolution.

At long last, the gods tired of dice. Thereupon, they created many creatures to be their playing pieces and a world in which to play. Humans and elves and dwarves and lizardmen, goblins and ogres and trolls and demons.

Betimes they adventure, they gain victory, suffer defeat, find treasure or happiness, and finally they die.

The gods, watching them, are in turn happy and sad; they laugh and they weep.

In time, the gods most unexpectedly came to enjoy the doings of their playing pieces, to truly love the world they had created. It was their devotion to this world that first showed the gods that they had hearts.

True, the dice sometimes go ill, and failures come, but such is the way of things.

Into this world, there appeared one particular adventurer.

He was an unexceptional young man. His wits did not distinguish him, nor his talents, nor his birth, nor his equipment, nor anything.

He was just a human warrior, such as you might find anywhere.

All the gods liked him, but this did not presage great things for him.

He would not save the world.

He might not even change anything.

After all, he was just another pawn, such as you might find anywhere…

But this adventurer was a little different from the others.

He was extremely careful, always thinking of plans, acting, training, letting no opportunity pass him by.

He did not let the gods roll the dice.

He did not need birth, or talent, or cheats.

Such things were as rubbish to him.

Even the gods were in his eyes irrelevant.

But one day, the gods realized something.

He would not save the world.

He might not even change anything.

After all, he was just another pawn, such as you might find anywhere.

But he would not let the gods roll the dice.

Thus, even the gods did not know what this adventurer's fate would be.

His fight continues somewhere even now.

AFTERWORD

Hi, everyone. Kumo Kagyu here.

This book is hardly perfect, but I put everything I had into it. If you enjoyed reading it, I will be thrilled.

I want to start out with something very important:

The adventurer depicted in this book has had a great deal of training. Please don't try this at home (without the permission of your Game Master).

The "weirdo" known as Goblin Slayer came out of a simple question: What would a fantasy world be like if it were home to an adventurer who only hunted goblins? From that question came a seed, and I kept writing from that seed until I had a whole work on my hands, and now that work has turned into a novel...

Over the two years it has taken for this book to see publication, my life has been full of people who could only be here by fate or perhaps extremely good luck:

All those who were interested in the seeds planted by that first question.

All those who encouraged me to turn those ideas into a novel.

All those who reviewed the novel.

Without every one of you, I would not be where I am now. Thank you. From the bottom of my heart, thank you.

I could never have dreamed this book would be picked up for a manga version before it was even published. If life is like a box of chocolates, I certainly never knew I was going to get this.

Speaking of incredible things:

There is a type of game referred to as tabletop role-playing games (RPGs) or "pen and paper RPGs," because you play them with a pen, paper, and dice. I have played tabletop RPGs for more than ten years now and will continue to play them for the foreseeable future—and here I've gotten to write a novel about them. My debut novel, no less. If I were to go back in time and tell my younger self this was how things would go, he would never believe me.

To the many Player Characters who have lived and died, adventured and retired: I couldn't have done this without everything I learned from you. You have my profound gratitude.

I haven't had a chance to write acknowledgments until now, and there are more people to thank than I can even count...

First, to all the readers of the online version of this book. You were there for me when it all started.

To all the friends involved in creating this book, thank you for your encouragement and your critiques. Your efforts helped make this book what it is.

To everyone who has gamed with me over the last decade, thank you. Let's go zombie killing again sometime.

To Noboru Kannatuki, my wonderfully talented illustrator: All the characters are adorable. Yippee!

To Kousuke Kurose, who is responsible for the manga version of the book: Thank you so much for taking on this project.

To the editor who gave me so much guidance and to the entire editorial staff at GA Bunko.

To everyone I never even met who worked to publish and promote this book, thank you.

To Steve Jackson, Ian Livingstone, Gary Gygax, Dave Arneson, Ukyou Kodachi, and Kiyomune Miwa. *Sorcery!*, *Dungeons & Dragons*, and *Chaos Flare* changed my life.

And finally, to everyone reading this book. Thank you so much. I hope to meet you someday—I can't wait.

Till next time!

Kumo Kagyu